Scandal in Silk: A Victorian Love Affair

Maryse Dawson

Published by Maryse Dawson, 2024.

This is a work of fiction. Similarities to real people, places, or events are entirely coincidental.

SCANDAL IN SILK: A VICTORIAN LOVE AFFAIR

First edition. May 7, 2024.

ISBN: 979-8231405404

Written by Maryse Dawson.

Also by Maryse Dawson

Pirates Quest
Tides of Desire (Pirates Quest Book 1)
The Pirates Quest Collection
Captive to the Heart

Standalone
Taming the Willful Miss Roberts
Between Duty and Desire
Scandal in Silk: A Victorian Love Affair
Lily's Christmas Promise
A Passion for Annie

Chapter 1

Cranleigh, Surrey 1878

The grand doors of the finishing school closed behind twenty-one year old Isabella Hamilton, marking the end of two years of refinement and education. She had emerged from the formidable institution as a proper young lady, or so one would think. A wicked smile lit up her face, for she knew that deep within her heart, the wild and untamed spirit still lingered.

With her final exams completed and her diploma in hand, Isabella's mind was filled with excitement for her future. She had no idea what lay ahead, but one thing was for sure: it was going to be a lot more exciting than the last two years!

As she bid farewell to her classmates, her best friend, Lady Genevieve Pemberton, approached with a mischievous twinkle in her eye. Genevieve was graceful, composed, and always in tune with the expectations of society, but she too had the same underlying spirit as her own. The two had become inseparable during their time at school, finding solace in their shared wit and rebellious spirits.

"Isabella, I have a proposition for you," Genevieve whispered, her voice filled with excitement. "Why don't you come and stay at my family's estate for the summer? Now that we're free of this boring place, we can truly have fun together." She turned around and looked at the front of the imposing building, pulling a disapproving face.

Isabella's eyes widened with delight. The idea of spending the summer at Oakwood Estate, surrounded by the magnificent gardens and elegant halls, was nothing short of a dream. She had visited before, but only for short durations, and had enjoyed every minute.

"Do you mean for the whole of summer?" she asked.

Genevieve nodded, her eyes alight with excitement. "Your parents won't mind, will they?"

Isabella laughed. "I very much doubt it. I expect they'll be glad for the peace. Being an only child, I think they feel I'm a bit of a whirlwind when I'm at home." She slipped her arm through her friend's and, grinning, said, "I accept your invitation wholeheartedly. We shall make this summer one to remember."

"Oh, I'm so happy you accepted. Now, go home, pack your best clothes, and come to Oakwood when you're ready. I'll be waiting!"

Isabella's heart fluttered with anticipation as she made her way to Oakwood Estate a few days later. She was eager to see Genevieve, and the carriage ride through the picturesque countryside seemed to be taking forever. But finally, the majestic entrance appeared, and her carriage trundled past the large ornate gates towards the house.

As the carriage rolled to a stop in front of the impressive estate, Isabella's eyes widened in awe. Oakwood Estate never failed to impress; it was such a beautiful house. Its fine stone pillars stood against a magnificent white facade, full of grandeur and elegance. The sweeping gardens, meticulously manicured, were full of pretty flowers and shrubs, and large, majestic trees dotted the landscape. Some were so ancient that she wondered what sights they must have seen—if only they could talk!

The driver opened the carriage door, and she stepped out gracefully onto the gravel driveway. Genevieve, dressed in a flowing gown of pale blue silk, stood at the entrance of the house, her face beaming with joy. She ran lightly down the wide stone steps and warmly embraced her. "Isabella! You've finally arrived!" she exclaimed.

"Oh, it's so lovely to see you, Genevieve. Your house looks so beautiful. I can't believe it's been six months since I was last here!" Isabella replied, her gaze sweeping over the estate's facade.

"Oh, yes, the Christmas ball! That was fun. But there will be summer balls to attend; don't forget."

"Thank you for inviting me, Genevieve."

Genevieve laughed, her musical voice filling the air. "Oh, my dear Isabella, I'm so excited that you're here. This summer will be like no other. Now, let's get you settled in your room. I've taken the liberty of preparing the grandest guest suite just for you."

Isabella followed Genevieve up the steps and through the large entrance, her eyes taking in the opulence of the interior. The walls were adorned with exquisite artwork and ancestral portraits; the furniture was elegant; and the chandeliers bathed the halls in a soft, golden glow. It was a world far removed from Isabella's modest upbringing, and she couldn't help but feel a sense of wonder.

As they ascended the grand staircase, Isabella's footsteps echoed along the corridor until, finally, they reached the door to Isabella's guest suite. Genevieve swung the door open, revealing a room fit for a princess. The sunlight streamed through the large windows, casting an inviting glow on the plush furnishings and delicate lace curtains. Isabella's eyes widened in delight, and she exclaimed, "Genevieve, this is absolutely lovely! Are you sure it's alright for me to stay in these rooms?"

Genevieve smiled, her eyes sparkling with excitement. "Of course it is, silly! And I'm thrilled that you love it." She turned around as the footmen began to bring in Isabella's luggage, and she showed them where to put them. A maid quickly appeared, and Genevieve pointed at the bags and said, "Put away Miss Hamilton's clothes, if you would, Sara, and then help her with anything she needs."

Genevieve grinned at Isabella. "Sara will be your personal maid for the duration of your stay. Now, freshen up and join me in the garden for tea. We have much to catch up on, and I simply cannot wait to introduce you to everyone."

With that, Genevieve left Isabella to settle into her new surroundings. Isabella took a moment to breathe in the scents of the room and then set about helping Sara unpack. The maid tried to get her to stop, but Isabella was insistent.

She wasn't used to having a personal maid. Yes, they had a couple of servants at home, but they mainly looked after the housekeeping. Personal maids were not something she was accustomed to.

As Sara helped her change into a fresh gown and brushed her hair, she couldn't help but be a little bit nervous about who Genevieve's other guests were. She had already met Genevieve's parents before, but who were the other people? It was all very exciting and a little bit nerve-racking!

Isabella stepped into the sunlit garden and looked around, wondering where Genevieve was. In the distance, she could hear the cheerful murmur of voices carried through the air and the occasional clinking of teacups. The sound of laughter and animated conversation told her exactly in which direction she needed to go!

Smiling with anticipation, she headed off towards the noise, almost running in her haste to join her friend and start the first day of her sojourn. It was so exciting! The sky was blue, the fields were green, and best of all, she was going to be spending time with her best friend.

Still looking up at the sky, she rounded the corner of the house and collided straight into a large force.

"Oh!" She gasped, slightly taken aback by the impact.

She would have fallen if it were not for the strong hands that reached out and settled on her upper arms. Looking up, she found herself staring at a strikingly handsome man.

A shiver ran down her spine as their eyes met. There was something undeniably captivating about him—an air of authority and masculinity. His dark hair was neatly combed, and his attire spoke of wealth and sophistication. But it was the intensity in his eyes that held her captive, as if he could see through her very soul.

"Are you alright?" he asked, concerned. His deep brown eyes gazed down at her with a hint of amusement.

"I beg your pardon; I didn't see you." Isabella said apologetically.

"Perhaps you should pay more attention to where you're going, rather than the sky." He suggested, dropping his hands. "It wouldn't do for you to take a tumble." He raised an eyebrow, hinting that she should be more careful.

She blushed hotly under his gaze. "No, indeed, and, um, thank you for your assistance."

"I should introduce myself," he said, smiling. "Lord William Somerset."

He bowed eloquently. Good grief, he was handsome! She quickly told him her name, "Miss Isabella Hamilton, my lord."

"I'm very pleased to meet you, Miss Hamilton. Now, if you'll excuse me." He gave her a brief nod and walked away, leaving her standing there in a daze. Coming to her senses, she shook her head. What was wrong with her? She'd seen handsome men before. But then never *that* handsome! She caught her breath and carried on the path towards her friend.

Lord Somerset smiled to himself as he strode towards the stables to retrieve his horse. The encounter with Miss Hamilton had made him wish he didn't have to leave so soon. But leave he must. He had business in town and had no time to dally. Although the exquisite beauty of Miss Hamilton had given him pause to regret his pre-planned meeting.

Her little heart-shaped face and intelligent blue eyes had made quite an impact. As brief as their meeting had been, he knew that he wanted to know more about her.

But he was a man of his word, and even a pretty face wouldn't dissuade him from his duty, as tempting as those soft blue eyes were.

Mounting his horse, he urged the big thoroughbred into a trot and was soon leaving Oakwood and galloping towards town.

Isabella finally spotted Genevieve sitting at a small wrought-iron table, her porcelain teacup delicately held between her fingers. There were several other tables, and the air was lively with their chatter. Isabella quickened her pace, excitement bubbling within her.

"Isabella, there you are!" Genevieve exclaimed, her eyes lighting up as Isabella approached. "Come, take a seat. The tea is freshly brewed, and the cook has prepared some delicious pastries and sandwiches."

Isabella took a seat opposite Genevieve and accepted a cup of tea, quickly helping herself to a small sandwich. "I confess, I'm quite famished. I hardly ate anything at breakfast. I was too excited to see you!"

Genevieve grinned. "And now you're here, my dear." She picked up a small pastry and sighed. "I missed these pastries when we were at school." She pulled a face. "I know the food wasn't bad, but it hardly compared to home. I'm glad school's finished, aren't you? Now we can have some real fun!"

Isabella giggled, her eyes dancing with amusement. "Oh, it was a bind. But I did get to meet you, so it wasn't all bad." She took a sip of tea before asking, "So, have you got anything planned for our first week?"

Genevieve's eyes twinkled. "Indeed, I have! How well you know me. Tomorrow, there's a ball being held in the Assembly rooms, and I've already made arrangements for us to attend. We should get there by eight, not too early and not too late. That way, we'll be noticed. And you know me, I like to be noticed!"

"And tell me, will there be any suitors there to capture your heart?" Isabella asked with a glint in her eye.

Genevieve's smile faltered for a moment whilst she pondered Isabella's words. "Well, in all truth, there's never been anyone that interested me. They're all too predictable, too consumed by their own egos. I long for something more, something that sets my heart ablaze." Her eyes suddenly lit up with devilment. "But this is a new summer, a new beginning, and perhaps we'll find ourselves with a multitude of suitors!"

Isabella nodded enthusiastically. "Now that would be fun!" A vision of Lord Somerset came into her mind, and she said, "Talking of men, I met Lord Somerset earlier. He's one very handsome man."

"Oh, indeed he is. But perhaps a trifle foreboding. He's a man of few words, but he possesses a reputation for his piercing insight. They say he can unravel even the most carefully crafted facade and see straight to the heart of a person."

Isabella's heart quickened at the thought of someone who might be able to see beyond her polite exterior to the untamed girl within. She had sensed that when she bumped into him.

Genevieve noted her silence and asked, "Do you like him?"

Isabella flushed, "If you mean do I find him attractive, then yes. Who wouldn't? But someone of his standing in society would never be interested in me. I have no title."

"So!" Genevieve said indignantly, "You're Isabella Hamilton, one of the prettiest and nicest girls I've ever known." She stopped for a moment sand then, giggling, added, "And one of the naughtiest, but we won't mention that!"

Isabella laughed. "You're just as naughty. I think whoever decides to marry us will need to know how to handle us."

"It won't be easy." Genevieve laughed. "Now, when you've finished, I'll take you around and introduce everyone to you. You'll be seeing a lot of them over the summer." She passed her another pastry, and Isabella happily took the tasty offering.

One thing was certain, Isabella thought happily as she looked around, spending time at Oakwood this summer was going to be anything but boring.

Isabella awoke the next morning and stretched her arms above her head. The bed was so comfortable that she felt no desire to leave it. She rolled onto her side and tucked her hands under her head whilst thinking about the previous day. Most of the people she'd been introduced to were relatives, and all had been very welcoming. The others were friends, and again, most of them seemed nice, but one girl had appeared rather haughty, and she'd sensed a feeling of hostility. Although she wasn't sure why, but some people didn't need a reason.

Isabella had asked Genevieve about her later, when they were alone. She was the same age as them, twenty-one, and Genevieve had confessed that she'd never taken to her. She was the daughter of a family friend, and no matter how many times they'd seen each other over the years, they had never gelled.

Her name was Victoria Grenville, and Isabella made a mental note to avoid her if possible.

A knock came on the door, and Isabella called out, "Enter."

It was Sara, and she was carrying a pitcher. "Morning, Miss. I've got some hot water for you, and Miss Genevieve has given you a lovely assortment of soaps."

She placed the pitcher on the stand next to the water basin and began to lay out various soaps. "My favourite is the rose, but there's lavender, verbena, and jasmine as well."

"Oh, how thoughtful." Isabella slid her legs from beneath the bed covers and padded over on her bare feet to see what she had. Choosing the jasmine, she was soon washed and dressed. Her long blonde hair had been neatly pinned up into an elegant knot, and she was ready for breakfast.

Genevieve poked her head around the door and smiled. "Oh, good, you're up. We can go down to breakfast together. Did you sleep well?"

Isabella nodded, "Like a log."

They linked arms and descended the wide staircase, chattering excitedly about the forthcoming ball and what dresses they were going to wear. Genevieve's parents were still at the breakfast table. Her father, engrossed in the latest tabloid, momentarily glanced up to murmur a morning greeting before returning to his reading. Her mother, peering over her spectacles, beamed with warmth as she welcomed the girls. "How are you settling in, Miss Hamilton?" she asked.

"Very well, thank you." Isabella replied, smiling.

"Excellent. Help yourself to breakfast; there's plenty to go around." She turned to Genevieve. "I've had a letter this morning from Lady Davenport. Apparently, we have a new neighbour."

"Oh!" Genevieve exclaimed, "has Linden Hall finally been sold?"

Her mother nodded, her eyes glinting with excitement. "Yes, three weeks ago, to a man of high standing, dearest, Lord Henry Worthington." She leaned nearer and, in a low voice, added, "And he is unmarried!"

Genevieve's father rustled his newspaper, and, lowering it, he looked at her mother. "Stop trying to matchmake, my dear. For all we know, he may be of dubious character. We know nothing about him."

Genevieve's mother straightened her shoulders and said indignantly, "I know very well that he is of good character. Lady Davenport says so herself in her letter. She picked it up and read aloud, "*He is a man who possesses a refined demeanor and distinguished countenance. He has maturity and wisdom far beyond his years. I believe you will find that he will make a wonderful neighbour and I think it a wonder, my dear, that such a man of distinction remains unclaimed by the bonds of wedlock."*

Genevieve pulled a face. "Then there must be something wrong with him? Is he old?"

"Thirty-two."

"Ugly?" She glanced at Isabella and pulled a face. "Maybe he resembles a gargoyle!"

Her mother laughed, "I haven't set eyes on him yet, dearest, so I cannot say. Apparently, he is an acquaintance of Lord Somerset, although I've never met him. I can only assume that he moved in different social circles to us." She took a delicate sip of her tea before adding, "But that is all about to change, my dears, for he'll be attending the ball tonight. So you'll be able to find out for yourself what he looks like."

Genevieve shot a wicked look at Isabella. "This evening just became a little more exciting!"

Cranleigh Assembly Rooms

Isabella and Genevieve stepped into the ballroom at the assembly rooms, their eyes widening at the sight before them. It had been beautifully decorated with no expense spared; ornate chandeliers cast their warm light onto the polished parquet flooring, and the lively music filled the hall, where already many elegantly dressed guests were twirling across the dance floor.

"Oh, this is lovely!" Genevieve grinned. "There are so many people here. I think we won't be short of dance partners, Isabella."

Isabella's heart skipped a beat as she spotted Lord Somerset across the room. His stern countenance only heightened his allure, and she couldn't help but feel drawn to him. She watched as he conversed with a group of gentlemen, his eyes occasionally scanning the crowd. He was so handsome.

Suddenly, as if sensing her perusal, he turned his face to meet hers. She blushed profusely at being caught staring and quickly looked away. Oh, lord. How embarrassing!

Genevieve, on the other hand, seemed captivated by the presence of another man. She grabbed Isabella's arm and, leaning near her ear, whispered. "I wonder if that's Lord Worthington?"

Isabella looked over to see a tall and rather dashing figure with a charming smile that he was currently directing at Genevieve's mother. "Do you think that could be him?" Isabella whispered.

Genevieve nodded and then giggled, saying, "Not so much a gargoyle, is he?"

"Indeed not!"

"We cannot lose this moment. Make haste; we must be introduced!"

Quickly, but without drawing attention, they crossed the room to join Genevieve's mother. "Oh, my dears, I'm so glad you're here." She exclaimed, and then, turning to the gentleman before her, she said, "Lord Worthington, may I introduce my daughter, Lady Genevieve, and her friend, Miss Isabella Hamilton."

He bowed politely and smiled warmly. "How lovely to meet you. I hope both of you will honour me with a dance this evening."

"Of course. We have come here with the intention of dancing the whole night away, haven't we, Isabella?" Genevieve replied.

Isabella agreed, "Oh, yes, I intend to enjoy this event to the fullest!"

"Then perhaps you'll allow me the first dance." A voice spoke next to her. Startled, she turned around to find Lord Somerset in front of her, his hand outstretched. "Would you do me the honour, Miss Hamilton?"

His eyes were dark and intense, and Genevieve's words came back to her. Could he truly see into a person's character? Lowering her lashes and her heart fluttering nervously, she placed her hand delicately in his. His touch immediately sent a thrill coursing through her veins, and she valiantly tried to calm her emotions whilst he led her onto the dance floor.

The musicians began playing the first notes of a waltz, and Isabella and Lord Somerset began to move in perfect harmony. As they twirled across the dance floor, Isabella couldn't help but notice the intensity in his eyes when he looked at her. There was a strength about him that set her pulse racing.

Their dance was magical, and as the waltz came to an end, Isabella found herself quite breathless, her heart pounding in her chest. Lord Somerset's hand lingered for a moment longer than necessary, his gaze searching her face. She saw a flicker of something in his eyes, an undeniable attraction, but before she could decipher it, he stepped back, his stoicism returning.

"You dance extremely well, Miss Hamilton. If it is not too much to ask, may I have another dance later this evening?"

Isabella smiled. "I would like that, my lord."

His eyes crinkled, and he bowed. "Until later, then."

Isabella watched him walk away to rejoin his friends, her mind filled with questions as she tried to make sense of her feelings. She'd never felt such an instant attraction to a man before. There was something enigmatic about Lord Somerset, and she knew she would like nothing more than to see him again.

Helping herself to a glass of sweet-smelling punch from a nearby waiter, Isabella looked around for Genevieve. Her face lit up with delight when she saw her dancing with Lord Worthington. They looked beautiful together, and from the laughter she could hear, it seemed their conversation was going well. Her eyes grew soft with happiness.

"What're you so happy about?" snapped a voice next to her, bringing her straight out of her reverie. She turned her head to find Victoria Grenville by her side.

"I beg your pardon," Isabella asked.

"If you think, for one minute, that Lord Worthington has any interest in Lady Genevieve other than to pass the time away, then you're gravely mistaken."

"That's not a very nice thing to say."

"I only speak the truth." She looked over at them, her eyes full of mockery. "Lord Worthington has certain, oh, how can I say, certain leanings towards things that Lady Genevieve will never accept."

Isabella frowned, "Whatever do you mean?"

"Oh, it's not for me to say. I think you should warn her away from him, that's all. Her heart will only get broken, like so many others before her."

Isabella narrowed her eyes and asked, "How do you know all this?"

Victoria turned her gaze on Isabella, her eyes hard. "It happened to me."

"Oh," Isabella said, a little shocked. She wasn't sure what to say. Should she commiserate? Should she pry? Or would that be rude?

Victoria shrugged dismissively and, turning to leave, said, "Just warn her."

Isabella watched her go and chewed her bottom lip. Was Victoria just showing her jealousy, or was she actually speaking the truth? Isabella didn't know her well enough to make a decision, but she would talk to Genevieve about it as soon as she returned. The thought of her friend getting hurt wasn't something she would like to contemplate.

Chapter 2

A little while later, Genevieve returned to Isabella's side, her eyes sparkling and her face flushed from exertion.

"Oh, my, Isabella!" she exclaimed. "Lord Worthington is such a good dancer! I haven't had this much fun in ages."

Isabella grinned and handed her a small glass of punch. She accepted it gratefully and took a large gulp.

"Steady on, Genevieve." Isabella admonished her good naturedly. "At this rate, you'll pass out before the ball finishes!"

"Oh, I can handle it. Lord Worthington's exuberance has given me such a thirst!"

Isabella decided to tell her right away about Victoria's warning. She needed to know what the woman had said, and then Genevieve could make up her own mind.

Genevieve listened and then rolled her eyes. "She's so jealous; she thinks she can have Lord Worthington for herself."

"She seemed so sincere, though, Genevieve."

Genevieve waved her hand in the air dismissively. "I know her of old, Isabella. I'd take anything she said with a pinch of salt. I'm certainly not going to let her ruin my evening."

Isabella wasn't so sure, but for now, she would agree to disagree and just enjoy the ball as they had originally intended. Genevieve wasn't stupid, and if there was something odd about Lord Worthington, she'd find out in time. Although, what Victoria was insinuating about him, she truly had no idea.

As the night drew to a close, Isabella and Genevieve found themselves quite exhausted. They had danced with so many people that they'd lost count, although Lord Somerset and Lord Worthington had left a lasting impression on both of them.

This was Isabella's first ball of the season, and it had been so splendid that it gave her high expectations for the summer ahead. It was going to be delightful, especially if she could spend some time with the handsome Lord Somerset!

Grinning happily, the two girls stepped into the carriage with Genevieve's parents and headed for home.

The next day, a letter arrived for Genevieve whilst they were having breakfast in the dining room. She opened it quickly, nearly ripping it in her haste to read the contents.

"Oh my, Isabella! It's an invitation from Lord Worthington to dine with him at Linden Hall this very evening!" Her eyes sparkling happily, she added, "The invitation extends to you as well, Isabella! How wonderful," she said excitedly, waving the letter in the air.

"Are you certain you want me there, Genevieve? I think I would feel like an interloper."

"No, silly, of course not. Besides, he says that Lord Somerset will be there."

Isabella gasped. "You didn't mention that just now."

"No, I wanted to see your reaction." She grinned. "Go on, admit it, you're attracted to him! The way you two danced last night, well, I personally think you're made for each other."

Isabella couldn't help but smile. "He is rather lovely, but I'm not so sure he feels the same towards me."

"How can he not?" Genevieve smiled. "Now, I will hear no more doubts. It's settled. You're coming tonight, and that's that."

The invitation to dine at Linden Hall, the grand estate of Lord Worthington, was rather daunting to Isabella. On the other hand, Genevieve was quite relaxed about it and, in fact, was very eager to see Lord Worthington again.

Victoria's warning still worried Isabella, and she decided to make a mental note to watch Lord Worthington carefully that evening to see if there were any signs of anything dubious in his character. Genevieve was already smitten, so she might not see the warning signs. But Isabella would take it upon herself to protect her. After all, that's what friends are for.

That evening, dressed in their best gowns and with their hair beautifully swept up in the latest fashion, Isabella and Genevieve stepped out of the carriage in front of Lord Worthington's grand house.

"I haven't visited here in ages." Genevieve exclaimed. "The house always appeared a little intimidating."

"Who lived here before?" Isabella asked, looking up in awe at the imposing building.

"Lord Mountjoy. He was very old, and unfortunately, when he died, he had no heirs. So the place has been empty for some time—over a year, I believe! I wonder if the interior is still as opulent, or did the spiders take over and spin their webs everywhere?" She put her hands into claws and pounced on Isabella.

"Genevieve! Do you mind?" She knocked her hands away, smiling at her antics.

Laughing together, they made their way up the wide, imposing steps towards the large oak door, which was instantly opened by an elderly butler with rather piercing eyes. Their smiles faltered upon seeing his grim countenance.

"Good evening; welcome to Linden Estate." He drawled, his voice low and serious. He stepped back, and the girls walked into the large entrance hall.

Isabella looked around in awe. It certainly didn't look like a house that had been uninhabited for a year or more. Everything was gleaming.

"Oh, it's beautiful, isn't it, Isabella?" Genevieve whispered. "I think it's even grander than Oakwood."

"My name is Watkins." The butler said, "If you would like to follow me, Lord Worthington and his guests are waiting for you in the drawing room." Before waiting for their answer, he turned around and headed towards the back of the hallway.

Isabella shot a glance at Genevieve and pulled a face, whispering, "What an odd fellow!"

Genevieve sniggered under her breath. "Quickly, follow him before he disappears!"

They quickly set off after him and were soon shown into a lavishly adorned room. Four people were there, among them Lord Worthington, who commanded attention as he stood by the crackling fireplace engaged in an animated conversation with Lord Somerset. As the girls gracefully entered the room, their presence captured Lord Worthington's gaze, prompting him to divert his attention from the conversation and cast his eyes upon them. The lingering gaze he fixed on Genevieve didn't go unnoticed by Isabella.

"Ah, ladies, you have arrived. Welcome to Linden Hall." He said, walking over to them. "Let me introduce you to the others."

"This is Lady Beatrice Somerset, Lord Somerset's sister." A young woman, about their age, inclined her head and gave them a broad smile. Isabella instantly took a liking to her.

"Lord Somerset, you already know," he continued.

Isabella's breath caught in her throat as her eyes met Lord Somersets, and she smiled shyly and said, "Good evening, my lord."

He returned her smile, seeming to be genuinely happy they were there.

"And this is Lord Peter Stansfield. A friend of mine."

The man bowed politely, and although he smiled, there was something in his eyes that Isabella didn't like. She couldn't quite put her finger on it, but her instincts advised her to be cautious.

"Now, would you care for an aperitif before dinner?" Lord Worthington asked.

"Oh, yes, perhaps a small glass of port for me." Genevieve said.

"And for me also." Isabella said quietly.

He looked across to Watkins and raised his finger. The butler instantly obeyed.

When Watkins handed her the glass of port, Genevieve turned to Lord Worthington and said, "The house is beautiful, my lord. Did you have much work to do when you moved in?"

"I've had an army of servants working around the clock from the day I moved in. You should have seen the cobwebs!" he remarked, shaking his head, his eyes glazing at the memory.

Genevieve shot a knowing glance at Isabella, who stifled a giggle in response. "We did wonder about that, didn't we, Isabella?"

Isabella nodded and took a sip of her port. It was velvety smooth, and it evidently came from a far superior source than she'd tasted before. Lord Worthington was obviously a man with impeccable taste.

He proceeded to show them the new furniture he'd bought and regaled them with a few tales about the interior transformation. All the while, Isabella could feel Lord Somerset's gaze on her. It was a little disconcerting, as she was unsure of his true intentions, and she found herself torn between curiosity and caution. Was this mere politeness or a genuine attraction?

She glanced at him a couple of times during Lord Worthington's conversation and found his dark eyes assessing her. She couldn't help but flush under his scrutiny.

Lord Stansfield seemed to be focused on Lady Beatrice, and Isabella couldn't help but notice the way she held his gaze. Was there an understanding between them? He appeared to be rather a lot older than her, somewhere in his forties.

Her perusal was interrupted by Watkins appearing to announce that dinner would be served shortly, so they all followed him into the grand dining room. It was adorned with exquisite tapestries, glistening chandeliers, and a long, polished table set for an elaborate dinner. The flickering candlelight cast a warm, inviting glow in the room.

"Oh, this is splendid, my lord." Genevieve commented, sliding elegantly into the seat one of the servants held out.

Lady Beatrice readily agreed. "I said the same thing when I first saw it. He does have marvellous taste."

As the meal commenced, conversation filled the air, ranging from politics and literature to the latest societal gossip. Lord Worthington, proving to be an eloquent host, regaled them all with tales of his travels and shared his passion for collecting rare artifacts and books. Genevieve listened intently, her eyes hardly leaving his.

Isabella was seated beside Lord Somerset, and when dessert was served, she found herself drawn into a conversation with him alone.

"Are you enjoying your stay at Oakwood?" he asked.

"Oh, yes. The house is so beautiful. I visited once at Christmas, but this is my first summer here."

"You're here for the whole of summer, are you not?"

She nodded.

"Then I should like you to see my home, Thornfield Manor. I think you'll find it most pleasing." He smiled at her and said, "I'll send an invitation for you and Lady Genevieve to visit. My sister will be delighted to have some female company."

Isabella's heart fluttered with a mix of excitement and uncertainty. He must be interested in her; otherwise, why would he ask her to visit his home?

She swallowed hard and replied, "That would be lovely."

As the evening progressed, Isabella couldn't help but notice the subtle glances exchanged between Lord Worthington and Genevieve. His desire for her was evident, and from the looks on her friend's face, she could see it was returned.

As the dessert plates were cleared and the final toasts were made, Lord Worthington rose from his seat, his eyes fixed on Genevieve.

"Would you ladies like some tea served in the parlour? Or if you like, I give you leave to explore my house at your will."

Genevieve's eyes lit up. "I would love to have a look around."

"I thought you might. You seem very inquisitive." He laughed low. "Just don't go into the west wing."

"Oh?"

"It hasn't been finished yet, and I'd rather you don't see it in its current state. We gentlemen, will be in the study. I fancy a cigar and a brandy to round off the night. If you'll excuse us."

The men bowed eloquently and left the dining room. Lady Beatrice used their absence to also excuse herself and dash off to use the bathroom. Genevieve immediately turned to Isabella. "Oh my, Isabella! Did you see how attentive Lord Worthington was to me during dinner? I'm certain he likes me!"

"I think so too, Genevieve. I've been watching him, and I do wonder what Victoria was going on about. I think you were correct, and she is simply jealous."

"I'm sure of it. But enough about me. What about you and Lord Somerset? He can hardly take his eyes off you."

Isabella, her cheeks flushed with uncertainty, replied in hushed tones, "Oh, I cannot say for certain, Genevieve, although Lord Somerset has certainly been attentive."

"I think you and I are in for a summer of fun. Talking of which, come on, let's go and explore. I am dying to see the bedrooms."

"Shouldn't we wait for Lady Beatrice?" Isabella asked.

"She could be ages and besides, she's been here before. This is all new to us, and I want to snoop!"

They left the dining room and ventured up the sweeping staircase. Ancestral portraits hung on the walls, the elegant men and women staring down at them imperiously, along with beautiful ornate paintings.

"He has very good taste, doesn't he?" Isabella exclaimed.

"Indeed, he does! That's why he likes me!" Genevieve laughed. "Oh, look, that must be a guest room."

They walked into a pretty bedroom whose door was ajar. The bed had silk drapes on the four posts, which matched the elegant curtains on the window. Genevieve ran her hand over the elegant covers and sighed. "So beautiful."

The next four bedrooms were similar. At the end of the corridor was an ornate wooden door, and Isabella eyed it with curiosity. "Do you think that leads to the west wing?"

Genevieve's eyes widened. "You're not suggesting that we...!"

"I am!" She placed a hand on her sleeve. "If he's hiding anything, it'll be here. Don't you want to put your mind at rest?"

Genevieve gave a wicked smile. "Yes!" Darting a look over her shoulder to make sure they were alone, she opened the door, and the two slipped inside.

The hall was darker than the rest of the house, and they waited a moment for their eyes to adjust to the dimly lit interior. Isabella looked around and frowned. "This is a little odd, don't you think?" she whispered.

"Very odd, indeed!" Genevieve replied in a hushed voice. "This is certainly not unfinished. In fact, it looks quite plush."

They ventured forward up the dimly lit hallway until their eyes fell upon a door that was slightly ajar. A soft glow emanated from within, and curiosity overcoming caution, they gently pushed the door open, revealing a small library bathed in the warm glow of candlelight.

Isabella looked at Genevieve, silently asking if they should continue. She nodded emphatically, both of a like mind. Bookshelves lined the walls, filled to the brim with leather-bound volumes, their spines marked with titles written in gold print. The two girls exchanged a nervous glance, their hearts pounding with anticipation. The books looked expensive and were hardly touched.

"We shouldn't be doing this, should we?" Genevieve whispered. "But I can't help myself now that I'm here!"

"If we're quick, he's not going to find out." Isabella reasoned, "Come on, I want to see what these books contain."

"What if there's a spider on one of them? I'll scream!"

"No, you won't!" Isabella hissed, "Unless you want Lord Worthington to hear you and find out we've been spying!"

Isabella hurried over to one shelf and quickly pulled out a slim book.

Taking it to the desk in the centre of the room, she flipped open the cover and began leafing through the pages.

"Oh, my!" She breathed, her eyes growing wide with shock.

"Oh!" Genevieve exclaimed. "That's indecent!"

Suddenly, the sound of footsteps reverberated through the corridor, shattering the silence. Fear gripped them as they realized they were about to be discovered. Instinctively, Isabella shoved the book down her bodice. Panic-driven, they quickly hid themselves behind the heavy tapestry curtains by the window, their hearts pounding in their chests.

As the footsteps grew louder, Isabella reached for Genevieve's hand and squeezed it nervously. What if they were discovered? The books were scandalous, and she knew they'd stumbled upon something extraordinary. Oh, Lord, they were going to be in so much trouble if they were caught. Silently, they waited, praying they wouldn't be seen.

Through the gaps in the fabric, Isabella saw Lord Worthington himself enter the room. His footsteps were purposeful, and his eyes were scanning the room for any sign of intrusion. Isabella held her breath, praying that their presence would go unnoticed. She clutched Genevieve's hand even tighter, drawing strength from their shared determination.

Lord Worthington's gaze lingered in their direction for a moment, but he seemed to dismiss it as a trick of the shadows. Satisfied that all was as it should be, he left the room, closing the door behind him. Genevieve and Isabella released a collective sigh of relief, their hearts still pounding in their ears.

"Oh, lord, that was a close call!" Isabella whispered.

Genevieve laid a hand on her chest. "I thought he would surely hear my heart thumping!" She peered out properly into the room and, satisfied they were alone, quickly stepped out. "Come on, we have to get back without being noticed."

Isabella thought about putting the book back that was concealed in her bodice but she was curious to know what else lay within the other pages, so she kept it hidden. Genevieve opened the door quietly and looked out into the corridor, left and right. "It's all clear. Let's hurry."

They left the library with much haste, and they were soon back in the other part of the house. As they walked along the corridor, Isabella hurriedly ushered Genevieve into one of the bedrooms.

"I can hear someone!" Isabella said, "Quickly! Sit on that chair!" She pushed Genevieve down into the seat. Just as she did, Lord Worthington strode into the room.

He looked from one to the other, his eyes speculative. "I've been looking everywhere for you."

Genevieve spoke up, "We were in here."

"I can see that now, but you weren't here a moment ago." His voice had an edge of steel to it, and Isabella felt her stomach roil nervously.

Genevieve gave him a little laugh. "Oh, this is such a big house. Where did you think we would be?"

"I did wonder for a moment if you'd disobeyed me and wandered into the west wing." His eyes bore into hers.

"Of course we didn't. You told us not to." She stared at him with big eyes, and Isabella watched him warily, wondering whether he would believe her.

His face was set, and he didn't look particularly happy, but he appeared to accept Genevieve's excuse. "Very well. The west wing is a dangerous place to be at the moment; some of the floorboards need replacing. I was concerned for your safety and rather hoped that you hadn't defied me."

Genevieve stood up and walked over to him. "Of course we wouldn't do that."

He fixed her with a look and said, "I should hope not."

Isabella had a feeling that he really didn't believe them, but because he couldn't prove otherwise, he didn't follow it up. Thankfully.

His underlying hint of steel made her nervous and it was in that moment that Victoria's words came back to her. Maybe there was a hint of truth in her warning!

Chapter 3

The discovery of the scandalous books within the west wing at Linden Hall gave Isabella and Genevieve lots to talk about on the carriage ride home.

"That's why Lord Worthington didn't want us going into that part of the house." Genevieve reasoned. "Because, as far as I could see, there was nothing dangerous in there at all."

Isabella shook her head. "No, indeed. Just his secret library. I wonder if all the books are on this subject." With a bit of careful maneuvering, she pulled out the book she had thrust down her bodice and held it up to Genevieve.

"Oh, my! I didn't see you hide that!" She peered at the title in the dim light of the carriage. "*How to deal with an errant woman.*"

Isabella grinned and quickly opened it, holding it flat in front of her so they could both see. Their eyes widened simultaneously.

"He's spanking her!" Genevieve gasped. "Oh my! Turn the page."

The next drawing showed a woman with her hands tied to bedposts and her bare bottom in the air, receiving a beating from a man wielding a cane.

"Oh, lord. This reminds me of that book we read at finishing school. Do you remember? The one that Charlotte let us borrow." Isabella exclaimed.

"Oh, yes! That was very risqué, but this is on another level altogether. I mean, look at these drawings." Her eyes were practically popping out on stalks.

"Do you think all the books are like this? We didn't get long enough to explore properly. What does this say about Lord Worthington's character, though, Genevieve?"

Genevieve turned another page, and her jaw nearly hit the floor. This time, the man had his hands on the woman's hips and had his manhood penetrating her from behind.

"Good lord!" exclaimed Isabella. "Is that what a man's cock looks like? It's huge!"

"Cock? Where did you learn such language, Isabella?" Genevieve's eyes sparkled wickedly.

"The same place you did, dearest Genevieve! Between the lines of Charlotte's book. Don't act so innocent!"

She giggled and turned another page. As risqué and explicit as it was, neither of them could look away. At the end of the book, there was a paragraph.

"Let me read it," Genevieve asked. Taking the book in her hands, she read aloud, her voice trembling with excitement and intrigue. "*In these days of patriarchal dominance, one must strive to contain the whims of disobedient women. This book unveils the ancient wisdom that allows a man to reclaim his rightful place in the world.*"

"Rightful place?" Isabella huffed, "And what do they mean by disobedient? Having her own mind? Her own thoughts?"

"Do you think it hurts?" Genevieve said, wide-eyed.

"What?"

"Being punished like that?"

Isabella pulled a face. "Well, it must do. Madame Beauvoir rapped me over the knuckles once with her ruler, and that hurt like hell! Didn't you ever get that?"

Genevieve shot her a look of superiority. "No, but then I was never as poorly behaved as you," she giggled. "If you met a man like this," she pointed at the book, "you'd be getting that every day!"

"Cheek!" Isabella snatched the book out of her hands. "I've got a good mind to keep this from you now. You don't deserve to see it again."

"Oh, fie! I shall get another one when I next visit Linden Hall."

"What? You would dare to sneak into the west wing again!"

Genevieve nodded. "Of course! I'd have to be careful, but I really, really want to know what else lies hidden on those shelves!"

"What if he catches you? Aren't you scared?"

"Oh, I'll be careful. Very careful." She looked at her friend intuitively and said, "Don't tell me you don't feel the same. I know you, Isabella, and you are just as intrigued as I am."

Isabella shrugged her delicate shoulders. "Well, I can't help feeling a little bit curious."

"You see!" Genevieve tapped a finger on her mouth and said, "We just need another invite to Linden Hall now."

The carriage came to a halt outside Oakwood, and the two girls stepped out onto the gravel driveway, feeling quite overwhelmed but excited. The evening had proved to be far more interesting than either of them would have believed!

Linden Hall

Lord Worthington sipped on his brandy and stared across at Lord Stansfield. They were alone, the other guests having already departed.

"What did you think of Lady Beatrice and Miss Hamilton?"

Lord Stansfield pondered slowly, "I think there's an underlying rebellious streak in both of them. I can see it in their eyes. But I would say that Miss Hamilton is a little too determined for my tastes, whereas Lady Beatrice has all the right traits. She would be easy to manipulate."

Lord Worthington laughed, "I thought so too. The same goes for Lady Genevieve. I had Watkins follow her, and he confirmed she went into the west wing along with Miss Hamilton." He took a sip of brandy, smiling to himself. "So I went in there myself. I knew they were hiding behind the curtains, but I pretended not to notice. When I confronted them later, they lied so easily."

"They're certainly a pair of audacious young women. All three of them are. But I think Beatrice and Genevieve are perfect for what we're looking for." Lord Stansfield stated. "Beatrice held my gaze several times during dinner, so I believe there's an attraction between us."

"Then I shall invite them over again, but this time we'll catch them red-handed and give them an offer they cannot refuse!"

Lord Stansfield raised his glass. "To many delightful evenings!"

Thornfield Manor

Lord Somerset observed his sister from the opposite side of the breakfast table. His butler, Parkin, had just handed her a letter, and while reading the contents, he noted that her cheeks had become a little flushed.

"Who is the letter from, my dear?" he asked.

Beatrice chewed her bottom lip before replying, "Lord Worthington. He has invited me to dinner on Thursday evening."

"And whom else shall be present?"

"Lord Stansfield and Lady Genevieve."

"I see." He went quiet and tapped his fingers on the table. There was something about Lord Stansfield that he didn't like. Beneath his charming facade, he sensed a hint of cruelty. A man of dubious character and the thought of his young sister being in his company again didn't sit well with him at all. He'd seen the way Lord Stansfield had looked at her before, and last night had been no exception. He also noted the way Beatrice had responded. She was young and impressionable, and without his guidance, anything could happen.

"I don't think you should go. In fact, I forbid it."

Beatrice's eyes widened. "But why?"

"Lord Stansfield is a lot older than you and...!"

Beatrice stood up, her hands balled into fists by her side. "So? What does it matter to you? Just because you're my brother, don't think you get to choose whom I see."

"I'm your guardian, and it's my duty to ensure your safety. I'm not certain of Lord Stansfield's character, so yes, I forbid you from going."

"But that's not fair!" Beatrice moaned, pushing her bottom lip out sulkily.

"Fair or not, you will obey me. Do you understand?" His eyes bore into hers.

She sat back down with a thud and rolled her eyes, clearly annoyed but knowing it was futile to argue with him.

"If you like," he said, attempting to lighten the mood, "we can take a ride out this afternoon. You can ride the new mare, Empress."

She immediately perked up. "I'm not forgiving you, but the idea of riding Empress is too appealing to be cross with you for too long." She smiled reluctantly. "Besides, there will be other opportunities where I can meet Lord Stansfield."

"Only when I'm present." He declared, raising an eyebrow in warning.

"Of course, brother dearest. Now what time do you want me to be ready for our ride?"

Underneath the warm embrace of the afternoon sun, Isabella and Genevieve found themselves galloping across the rolling countryside, their horses' hooves rhythmically pounding against the earth. Laughter spilled from their lips, carried away by the gentle breeze tousling their hair.

Isabella loved to ride; it always gave her a sense of freedom and excitement—a carefree moment in time. As she traversed the verdant landscape, her eyes feasted upon the picturesque scenery that unfolded before her. The vibrant colors of wildflowers stood out against the backdrop of distant rolling hills.

Slowing their horses down to a gentle trot, the girls caught their breath. "It's been ages since I last rode a horse." Isabella noted, patting her horse's neck. "It's a shame we weren't allowed to ride at the finishing school."

Genevieve pulled a face. "I know, but I intend to make up for it now." She leaned back a bit in the saddle and allowed her horse free rein. "I feel bad about the invitation to Linden Hall. I'm not sure why Lord Worthington didn't include you in the invite."

"I think we know, Genevieve. He just wants you to himself, and as for Lord Stansfield, from what I observed, he's taken a liking to Lady Beatrice. Hence her invitation." She frowned. "Although, I do wonder at his interest in her, seeing as she is far younger than him."

"I find that age has no barriers. Besides, he is very handsome."

"Handsome, yes, but as to his character, I'm not certain. There is something about him that I don't like."

"I can't say I noticed." Genevieve shrugged her shoulders, "Maybe you're too critical of him?"

"Maybe. Time will tell. But truly, Genevieve, I shall be quite happy having a peaceful evening at home. I'll immerse myself in your library; you know how I love to read." Suddenly, Isabella gasped and reined in her horse.

Genevieve immediately did likewise. "What is it?"

"Look!" She pointed into the distance.

Genevieve glanced at the brow of the hill and saw two riders. One was clearly Lord Somerset. He was astride a magnificent steed, gazing upon the view.

"Oh, my," breathed Isabella, feeling her cheeks grow hot. "I didn't think we'd get to meet again so soon! Who is he with?"

Genevieve peered harder. "Why, it's Lady Beatrice. I wonder if she's received her invite to Linden Hall yet?"

"Do you think we should go and say hello?"

"Of course! It's the perfect opportunity for you to talk to Lord Somerset again. Come on, I'll lead the way."

With a mixture of curiosity and trepidation, Genevieve and Isabella approached the hill, their horses slowing to a gentle trot. Lord Somerset was the first to notice them, and his eyes showed a mix of surprise and pleasure.

His gaze lingering on Isabella, he offered a slight nod of acknowledgment. "Lady Genevieve and Miss Hamilton, what a pleasant surprise."

Isabella's cheeks flushed a delicate shade of pink as she returned his gaze.

Lady Beatrice grinned at the two girls. "How wonderful! It seems fate has brought us together once again. Perhaps we should take advantage and sit awhile." She looked from them to Lord Somerset. "Can we take a moment?"

Lord Somerset inclined his head and smiled. "I have no objection."

In no time, they found themselves seated on the grassy hillside, their horses leisurely grazing in close proximity. Lord Somerset chose to sit next to Isabella, while Beatrice sat near Genevieve.

Genevieve wasted no time engaging Beatrice in conversation. "I wanted to ask, have you received an invitation to Linden Hall?"

Beatrice's face fell, and, eyeing her brother sulkily, she said, "Yes, but I'm not allowed to go."

Genevieve gasped, looking over at Lord Somerset. "Why ever not?"

"There are many reasons, and I have no desire to explain. Please just accept that I forbid it." Lord Somerset said.

"Oh." Genevieve's eyes widened a little at his brusque manner, and Isabella noticed that she didn't attempt to pursue the matter. "I see. Well then, Beatrice, would you care to walk with me around the large tree over there?"

Beatrice immediately nodded, and rising up, the pair of them wandered off. Knowing Genevieve, Isabella realised she would be interrogating Lady Beatrice to find out the gritty details of her brother's objection.

Left alone, Isabella darted a glance at the man in question. He looked even more dashing than the last time she'd seen him. His dark, wavy hair glistened in the sun, and she had a sudden compulsion to run her fingers through it. Surprised at her scandalous thoughts, she quickly looked away, pretending to have an interest in the pretty scenery.

"So how do you and Lady Genevieve know one another?" Lord Somerset asked her, breaking into her thoughts.

"We met at finishing school." Isabella smiled, remembering their first encounter. "The first time was when we got caught creeping back into the building after midnight. Genevieve and I weren't as quick as the other girls, and the headmistress caught us red-handed!"

"Were you punished?"

Isabella looked into Lord Somerset's eyes and noticed a spark of curiosity. She felt her cheeks blush hotly under his scrutiny. "Yes, she wouldn't let us go to the country fair that week." Isabella's bottom lip pouted at the memory. Darned harridan!

She glanced back to find Lord Somerset looking amused, and he remarked, "I presume it taught you a valuable lesson on how to behave?"

Her eyes darkened a little, and she replied, "No, not really. I usually just find another way around things to get my own way."

"You have quite a defiant streak, don't you?" he observed, eyeing her speculatively.

"Not always, but it can come in useful." She raised her chin defiantly, wondering if he was going to give her a lecture on how to behave. Luckily, he refrained. It seemed to amuse him more than anything.

Genevieve and Beatrice returned, both looking quite excited and had obviously been planning something. Isabella looked from them to Lord Somerset to see if he noticed their demeanor.

"Lord Somerset, would you allow Beatrice to come to Oakwood on Thursday?" Genevieve asked him.

He raised an eyebrow and said, "What about your invitation to Linden Hall? That was on Thursday, was it not?" he asked.

Genevieve waved her hand in the air dismissively. "Oh, I've decided to decline. Without Lady Beatrice there, it would be meaningless. So I'd rather have your sister visit my own home, and then the three of us girls can have a lovely evening together."

Lord Somerset stared at her for a moment before standing up. He offered Isabella his hand. She placed her small hand in his gracefully and he helped her to her feet but rather than let her hand go, he raised it to his lips and kissed her knuckles.

The impromptu kiss had surprised Isabella so much that she didn't move for a moment, her heart fluttering with nervous excitement.

Lord Somerset turned to his sister. "I can see no reason why you cannot go to Oakwood but let me tell you now." He raised his finger in warning at Beatrice, "If I find out that you've disobeyed me and dined at Linden Hall, there will be consequences. Mark my words."

Isabella felt her stomach tighten at his words, and she saw the flush that stole over Lady Beatrice's face. She would be foolish to disobey him, but knowing Genevieve's character and her persuasive nature, if they'd made a plan, it would go ahead regardless.

Lord Somerset turned to Isabella and said, "We must away. I bid you good day, Miss Hamilton." He nodded at Genevieve and waited for his sister to say her goodbyes.

When they'd departed, Isabella turned to Genevieve and asked, "Beatrice isn't coming to yours, is she?"

Genevieve's eyes sparkled wickedly. "Of course she is, but it just so happens that we may visit Linden Hall during her visit!"

"Genevieve! What if her brother finds out?"

"He won't."

Isabella shook her head. "I wouldn't like to be in your shoes if he does."

"You worry too much." Genevieve laughed. "Now, let's gallop home. I have a need to feel the wind in my hair."

Linden Hall

The candlelight cast an ethereal glow in the west wing of Linden Hall as Genevieve and Beatrice stealthily made their way through the dimly lit corridor. Their hearts pounded in their chests as they approached the secret library that Genevieve had discovered previously with Isabella.

Since finding the scandalous book, she had an insatiable desire to uncover even more secrets that lay within the small room.

Lord Worthington had given her his undivided attention during dinner, and Lord Stansfield seemed rather infatuated with Beatrice, something she appeared to reciprocate.

Now that the men had retired to the study for their brandy and cigars, Genevieve had taken the opportunity to ask if she could show Beatrice around. He had, of course, complied.

Her previous encounter with him had left a mark on her mind; the intensity of his warning to keep away from the west wing was still quite fresh, but she was too inquisitive to stay away. The allure of forbidden knowledge beckoned her forward.

As they reached the door to the library, Genevieve hesitated, her hand poised to turn the doorknob. Beatrice's eyes met hers, filled with a mixture of excitement and unease. They exchanged a silent nod, their resolve firm, and Genevieve pushed the door open slowly, revealing the room bathed in shadows.

Beatrice's eyes widened in awe as she followed behind Genevieve. When she stepped cautiously into the room, her senses heightened with anticipation.

"Are these the books you were telling me about?" she whispered, walking over to one of the tall bookshelves. She hiccoughed and clapped a hand over her mouth. "Lord, my head is spinning! I think I shouldn't have had that extra glass of wine!"

Genevieve sniggered quietly. "I did notice you gulping that last one down. I think Lord Stansfield was trying to get you a little drunk. To be honest, I feel quite dizzy myself."

Beatrice steadied herself against the bookshelf, giggling. "I think you might have to help me back down the stairs. But first, I want to see what these books are about for myself."

"Be warned, they're quite graphic!"

Beatrice reached for a book, and pulling it off the shelf, she laid it on the central table. When she opened the pages, her eyes widened in shock and swayed a little. "Oh, my, Genevieve. I've never seen anything like this!"

"I know. Heaven knows where Lord Worthington got them from. They are truly scandalous."

Beatrice turned over the pages one by one, her eyes widening with each drawing presented to her innocent eyes. Suddenly, she snapped the book shut and shook her head, immediately putting her hand out to steady herself. "We must leave at once, Genevieve. This feels wrong."

Genevieve went to reply when suddenly, the silence was shattered by the sound of the door creaking open. The girls both froze, their hearts pounding in their ears. Lord Worthington stood in the doorway, his eyes ablaze with a mix of anger and devilment.

"Ah, so you couldn't resist, could you?" Lord Worthington's voice dripped with a cold, calculated tone. "Even though I told you not to come here, you had to defy me."

Genevieve and Beatrice stood stock still, their faces pale with guilt and apprehension. They knew they had crossed a line, and now they would have to face the consequences of their actions.

Lord Stansfield stepped forward and rested his gaze on Beatrice, his voice seething with disdain. "And you, Lady Beatrice, I had hoped for better from you, but it appears that curiosity has clouded your judgment."

Beatrice's heart pounded, and she hiccoughed again, suddenly feeling most unwell indeed. The weight of Lord Stansfield's disappointment pressed upon her, and she realised that her curious nature may have just got her into a lot of trouble!

Lord Worthington approached them slowly, his expression unyielding. "These books are not meant for the likes of you, and I'll not allow you to reveal what I've protected for so long."

Genevieve summoned her courage, her voice trembling but firm. "My Lord, we apologize for trespassing. We were simply curious, that was all. And we won't tell a soul about your collection!"

Lord Worthington's eyes bore into Genevieve's, his anger momentarily softening. "Curiosity can be a dangerous path, my lady. It leads to unforeseen consequences. I find I cannot simply ignore what you've done."

"There is a way, however, to atone for your sins." Lord Stansfield said, looking from one girl to another.

Genevieve exhaled slowly and asked, "How?"

He stepped forward and looked at the open book on the table, his firm fingers flicking through the pages until he fell on a certain page.

Holding the book up in his hands, he tapped the picture and said, "Six of the best, my dears."

Genevieve and Beatrice gasped. The picture was of a young woman draped over a man's lap, her bottom bare, and receiving a spanking.

"You would spank us?" Genevieve breathed, her eyes wide.

"That's what happens to bad girls. You can either accept the consequences of your misbehaviour or you can leave Linden Hall and never set foot here again. The choice is yours." Lord Stansfield replied, his face stern and unyielding as he awaited their reply.

Chapter 4

As Genevieve and Beatrice returned home in the carriage later that night, they both sat silently contemplating what had just happened.

Beatrice had her eyes closed and was looking extremely pale. She had balked at the very idea of a spanking, and Lord Stansfield, noticing her palour, had rolled his eyes with disgust before ushering her back downstairs.

Whereas Genevieve had agreed and was now feeling a mixture of excitement and, dare she say, arousal! Her bottom was smarting from having received six stinging slaps to her bare backside from the very handsome Lord Worthington, and far from being embarrassed, she found she had enjoyed every moment of his attention.

He'd scolded her throughout, and she had squirmed with discomfort, but now she couldn't stop thinking about his large hands and firm physique. She picked up her fan and attempted to cool her blushing cheeks.

Beatrice opened her eyes and looked at her groggily. "I can't believe you went through with that, Genevieve!" she whispered.

"Me neither." Genevieve chewed her bottom lip. "But there was something exciting about the whole episode. Being caught and punished was quite... well, exciting!" She closed her eyes for a moment, "and Lord Worthington's thighs are so strong."

Beatrice pulled a face. "I found the whole episode humiliating! To think they could even suggest such a thing. I wish I hadn't drunk so much; my head is thumping." She groaned and added, "Maybe I should have listened to my brother?"

"Oh, piffle! What does he know?"

The carriage arrived back at Oakwood Estate, and the two girls made their way upstairs. Beatrice's ascent was a little slow, and Genevieve quickly gave her a helping hand by slipping her arm around her waist to give support.

"Oh, dear. My head is spinning so." Beatrice moaned softly.

"Next time, I think you would do well to drink only one glass of wine, dearest."

Beatrice pulled a face. "Or maybe none!"

Genevieve giggled softly. "Wise words."

They reached the top landing, and Genevieve whispered, "Shall we see if Isabella is still up?"

"Yes. I really need a glass of water. I have such a thirst."

Reaching Isabella's door, Genevieve knocked softly on the door. "Isabella? Are you awake?" She said it as quietly as possible, hoping not to awaken anyone else in the other bedrooms.

She heard rustling, and then the door opened a little to reveal Isabella in her nightgown, her hair in a plait.

"You were not asleep?" Genevieve enquired, looking a little sheepish. "I hope we didn't wake you."

"No, not at all. I was reading. Quickly, come in before we disturb anyone."

She opened the door fully and let them in, quickly noticing Beatrice's solemn expression.

"Did the evening not go very well?" she asked, frowning. "Would you like to sit down, Beatrice? You don't look at all well."

"She drank too much wine." Genevieve declared. "Which was Lord Stansfield's fault. I saw him refill her glass when she wasn't looking."

"Oh, dear. Come and sit on the bed, Beatrice." Isabella offered, taking her arm and guiding her over to the bed.

Beatrice sank into the comfortable mattress and lay back against the pillows. "Oh, my head is spinning so!"

"Eugh, I hope she doesn't throw up." Genevieve said, pulling a face.

Isabella threw her a look of rebuke. "Have some sympathy, Genevieve. I think we've all been in this situation at some point in our life!"

Genevieve had the grace to look humble and apologised. "I'm sorry. It's just been rather an eventful evening with one thing and another." She walked over to the side. "Is this water fresh? Beatrice said she was thirsty."

Isabella nodded, and before long, Beatrice was gratefully sipping on a glass of water.

Genevieve sat down on one of the comfortable chairs and began to recount the events that had unfolded in the library at Linden Hall.

When she'd finished, Isabella's eyes were wide with shock. "I cannot believe he actually spanked you!" she gasped. "I'm astonished not only that he demanded such a thing but that you actually complied!"

Genevieve, her eyes sparkling devilishly, added, "Isabella, I know it sounds awful and quite scandalous, but in all honesty, I would do it again."

"You would?" Isabella gasped.

Beatrice gave a small groan, and reaching out, Isabella placed her hand on her forehead. "You feel quite hot, dearest. I think we should get you to bed."

Beatrice's eyes fluttered open, and she squeezed Isabella's hand. "You won't tell anyone about tonight, will you?"

Isabella shook her head. "I promise I won't. Your secret is safe. I understand your reasons for exploring the library—why, I've even done it myself. So we're all as bad as one another."

Beatrice's eyes brightened with gratitude, and she whispered, "Thank you, Isabella."

Isabella smiled, and then, looking at Genevieve, she said, "Let's help Beatrice to her bedroom. I think we've had enough excitement for one night, don't you?"

Later that night, lying alone in her bed, Isabella couldn't help but worry about Genevieve and Beatrice. It was one thing to read a scandalous book, but being caught in the act was a dangerous game. A game that Genevieve had taken one step further by actually allowing Lord Worthington to spank her. Most certainly a step too far.

What if anyone discovered what had happened? Why, they could never show their faces in public again! And what man would want a woman sullied by such a scandal? And what sort of men were they that they would demand to do such a thing in the first place?

She rubbed her forehead and closed her eyes. Sleep was almost impossible, but eventually her troubled mind drifted off to a peaceful slumber.

The next morning, after breakfast, Isabella joined Beatrice and Genevieve in the rose garden. Making sure no one was around, Genevieve pulled out the book that Isabella had stolen from Lord Worthington's library.

Beatrice blushed fiercely when she caught sight of it. "Oh, my Genevieve. I didn't realise you had such a book in your possession!"

Genevieve giggled. "Isabella stole it from Lord Worthington's library."

Beatrice's eyes widened. "Oh, Isabella. How naughty of you!"

Isabella gave a wry smile. "That had just been a little fun, and I'm thankful I wasn't caught like you two were. I still cannot believe what happened." She shook her head. "Do you think this is why Victoria Grenville warned us about him?"

Genevieve pulled a condescending face. "Even if she had experienced the same thing, which I highly doubt, she's obviously far too much of an introvert to enjoy that side of life. I expect she's frigid!" She laughed scornfully.

Isabella immediately advised caution. "I do feel that you're playing with fire, Genevieve."

"Oh, Isabella, you need not worry so," Genevieve said with a wave of her hand. "I was merely curious. Besides, no real harm has been done.

Isabella remained unconvinced. "The sort of acts described in that book could ruin a lady's reputation if discovered. Think of how your family would feel, Genevieve, to know you were indulging in such scandalous behaviour."

For a moment, Genevieve looked troubled, but then, raising her chin, she said defiantly, "It's none of their business what I do. Besides, I only received a spanking. It was nothing really. Certainly not like those other pictures in the book! Good lord!"

"Indeed!" Isabella eyed the book nervously and said, "I think we should burn it or replace it at least. Don't you?"

Genevieve's eyes widened, and she clasped the book to her bosom, sending a reproachful look at Isabella. "No way! It's far too exciting to dispose of so readily."

Isabella went to say something, but Genevieve interrupted her, "I shall endeavour to ensure that no one, especially my family, ever hears a whisper of what happened."

"That would be wise." Isabella cautioned, "But I have to ask, do you intend for the same thing to happen again? Would you risk your reputation?"

Genevieve thought hard for a moment, "I know Lord Worthington's actions were rather unusual, to say the least, but he's the first man that's made my heart flutter." She sighed softly, "If he invites me again, I shall surely go. It's too exciting to turn down."

"Well, I can tell you now that I won't be going to Linden Hall again. I have no wish to see Lord Stansfield ever again. I found his behaviour unacceptable." Beatrice said.

"Wise words, Beatrice." Isabella noted.

Isabella was very glad that Beatrice had some common sense, but it seemed that Genevieve was unwilling to turn away from the lure of Linden Hall and the captivating Lord within. This wasn't exactly the summer she had envisioned.

Lord Somerset arrived with the carriage in the late afternoon to collect his sister. Isabella immediately noted the look of surprise on her face.

"Brother! What're you doing here?" Beatrice asked as he descended from his fine carriage. "I'd planned to take a carriage home alone after my visit."

"I thought it prudent to collect you myself," Lord Somerset replied with a meaningful look. "And I had hoped to extend an invitation to Miss Hamilton and Lady Genevieve to join us for dinner at Thornfield Manor this evening." He cast his gaze on Isabella, his eyebrows raised, waiting to see if she would accept.

Isabella's cheeks flushed pink at the sight of him, though she tried to remain composed. She turned to Genevieve and asked, "We have nothing planned tonight; do we, Genevieve?"

"No, indeed. We would be delighted to accept, my lord."

"Oh, that will be lovely!" Beatrice said with genuine happiness. "I shall return home with my brother. Will you stay for a day or two?"

"We would love to." Isabella responded readily. The thought of spending time with Lord Somerset was something she wasn't about to turn down!

"Then it is set. I'll send the carriage for you at eight." Lord Somerset said, smiling.

When they'd departed, Genevieve clutched Isabella's arm. "He likes you! It's so obvious!"

"He is so courteous and gentlemanly." Isabella smiled softly.

Genevieve laughed at the look on her face. "Come on, we must make haste and prepare for our visit. You simply must look your very best."

Isabella could hardly contain her excitement as Lord Somerset's carriage ferried them to Thornfield. She had worn one of her favourite dresses, a pale blue creation with lace and pearls, and her hair was neatly swept up into a pretty chignon with matching ribbons. Genevieve had declared that she had never seen her look so pretty.

Nervously, she stepped out onto the gravel drive, and when her eyes met Lord Somerset's, she knew without a doubt that her feelings were returned.

That evening, over a delicious meal, Lord Somerset was the perfect gentleman, attending especially to Isabella. Their lively conversation and easy rapport didn't go unnoticed by Genevieve and Beatrice, who darted knowing glances at each other.

With the last course served, Lord Somerset asked Isabella if he could show her around his house. Isabella happily accepted, of course. Time spent alone with him was something she'd been looking forward to.

He turned to his sister and said, "Perhaps you could show Genevieve the new piano, Beatrice?"

"Do you play, Beatrice?" Genevieve asked, "I tried to learn at finishing school, but I'm not very good."

"I love it. Come with me, and I'll teach you some easy pieces to play."

Lord Somerset led Isabella through spacious halls and corridors adorned with portraits of his past ancestors. Outside, through the upper-leaded windows, she could see the softly rolling green hills and grazing pastures. It was a beautiful estate.

"You have a beautiful house, Lord Somerset."

He stood beside her and looked out of the window. "Yes, it is beautiful. My father used to like sitting down there," he said, pointing to the stone terrace. "He'd write his journals and if anyone disturbed him, he would shake his cane at them!" He laughed at the memory.

"Your father is no longer here?"

He shook his head and said, "No. Unfortunately, he died ten years ago." His expression turned sad for a moment. "He succumbed to a fever one winter. It was a very sad time for both Beatrice and I."

Isabella hardly dare ask, "And your mother?"

"She died during childbirth a few years before that. The child never survived." He gave a long sigh. "Hence the reason I became Beatrice's guardian. She has no one else."

Isabella nodded. "I'm sorry for your loss, my lord, and I find it very admirable that you look after Beatrice so well. She has such a kind nature. I like her very much."

"As she does you. She often talks about you." He turned and looked at her, smiling.

Isabella couldn't help the blush that stole over her cheeks.

He held his arm out. "Would you care to take a walk with me in the gardens, Miss Hamilton? There is a viewpoint where we can watch the setting sun."

"Oh, that would be lovely. There is nothing prettier or more serene than a beautiful sunset."

Lord Somerset looked down at Isabella and had a moment to disagree. Her beauty alone was just as beautiful. He was finding her company even more pleasurable than he'd imagined. She had a lively mind, and beneath the surface, there was a wicked sense of humour. One that he hoped he would one day unleash.

Coming to a stone bench overlooking the rolling hills, Lord Somerset gestured for her to take a seat. She did so, her breath catching as he joined her, their hands mere inches apart.

As the sun dipped low in a blaze of orange and pink, he turned to her and said, "Miss Hamilton, I know we haven't known each other very long, but I find I have come to admire you greatly."

Isabella's soft blue eyes stared back at him shyly so he continued unabashed. "I wonder if you would allow me to court you?"

He watched her cheeks blush alluringly and reached out to take her hand, noticing how small and delicate her hand looked in his. "I will not rush you. Perhaps you need time to think about your answer."

"No, no. I will gladly accept your courtship for I also have come to admire you. I confess to being a little overwhelmed."

"Of course. Perhaps I should have given you more time, but I have felt a connection between us."

"I feel it too."

"Then it's settled!" He gave her a wide smile. "I shall escort you back to the house. I expect you are quite fatigued from all the excitement today." He stood up and offered her his arm. She arose gracefully and placed her hand on his sleeve.

As they walked back, he said, "I'd like to show you the stables tomorrow. Would you like to take a ride out? Or even better, we can have a picnic prepared. I know my sister would enjoy it, and I presume Lady Genevieve would too. I will invite my neighbours, Miss Eliza Harmon and her sister, Miss Margaret Harmon. Both elderly spinsters and extremely lovely ladies. You will like them, I'm sure."

They walked back together as dusk settled over the land and the tranquility of the night began to descend, talking quietly of the future to come. Isabella was more content than she had ever known.

The next day, with the weather being fine, Lord Somerset set about preparing for the picnic. They would ride out and have the blanket laid out on the hill, where the servants would lay out the food and drink. Shade would be supplied for those who needed it. It was going to be a splendid day.

Miss Eliza and Miss Margaret Harmon had already replied that they would love to attend. They had lived on the estate for decades, and Lord Somerset had always got along well with them. In his youth, they had often given him treats when he'd happened to pass by their house. Now that he was older, he liked to repay their kindness when he could.

In Isabella's opinion, it only elevated her feelings for the handsome man.

The servants packed baskets with all manner of delicacies, and the group set out. Much to Lady Beatrice's delight, the Harmons great nephew, Captain Jonathan Harmon, happened to be visiting and had happily agreed to join them. She'd only met him a couple of times, but found him very agreeable.

They climbed one of the grassy rises dotted with wildflowers, chattering and laughing all the way.

At the top, the elderly Harmon sisters stopped for a moment to catch their breath. Miss Margaret declaring that she wasn't as young as she used to be, and Miss Eliza reprimanding her jovially for not walking enough!

As they ate the variety of food set out on platters, Lord Somerset couldn't keep his eyes from Isabella. She seemed to glow with joy, fitting in so effortlessly with his family and friends. Genevieve, too, had become fast companions with the Harmons.

Suddenly, hoofbeats could be heard, and Lord Somerset looked up to find Lord Worthington and Lord Stansfield approaching them. He felt his body tense and inwardly groaned at the intrusion. He turned around to look at Isabella just in time to see a look of what he could only say was trepidation when she spied the two riders.

His eyes narrowed. What had made her react like that? What did she know?

Isabella glanced over at Genevieve to see if she'd seen Lord Worthington, but she was lying on her front, engrossed in showing Miss Margaret a book she was reading. It was only when he'd dismounted and stood over her, his shadow covering the page, that Genevieve realised he was there.

She quickly scrambled to a sitting position, her eyes wide. "Oh, Lord Worthington!"

He went down on his haunches and closed her book, his eyes scanning the cover. "Good afternoon, Lady Genevieve. I gather you like reading."

Isabella's eyes widened, and she almost held her breath. Surely he wouldn't reveal any secrets here? Would he? Oh, lord.

Her eyes darted to Beatrice, noting that her cheeks were suffused with colour. Lord Stansfield had also dismounted and came to stand next to Lord Somerset.

"Good afternoon, William. What a wonderful day it is, and to be having a picnic with such pretty company—I confess to being quite jealous!"

Isabella watched Lord Somerset's face darken a little, but he politely replied, "Would you care to join us?"

She could tell he would rather they didn't, but etiquette deemed him to allow them to join.

"How splendid of you."

Lord Stansfield immediately set his sights on Beatrice, taking a seat beside her and monopolizing her conversation immediately. Beatrice, who was seated between him and Captain Harmon, was doing her best to look calm, but Isabella knew she would be terrified he would reveal what had happened at Linden Hall. Not only that, but if her brother found out she'd gone against his wishes in the first place, she would be in a great deal of trouble. She felt just as worried herself!

Isabella decided to keep a watchful eye on both Beatrice and Genevieve as the afternoon continued, but with the new guests in attendance, it proceeded in a rather more subdued fashion.

Lord Somerset was certainly not happy at this turn of events. Not at all. His sister had been quite enthralled with Captain Harmon earlier, and yet now Lord Stansfield was doing his best to keep the attention on him. It didn't sit well with Lord Somerset at all.

With a discerning gaze, he recognized that Captain Harmon possessed far greater suitability as a match for his sister than the pompous Lord Stansfield. He was younger by several years, and he knew him to be a man of great character.

While skillfully maintaining the conversation between the Miss Harmons and Isabella, Lord Somerset remained vigilant, his attention subtly drawn towards his sister's interactions. A sense of protective concern gripped him. He also couldn't help but notice Isabella's frequent glances towards Beatrice and Genevieve. It would seem she too was perturbed by the change in ambience.

He had a lot of questions and one thing was certain: when he returned home, he would find the answers.

Chapter 5

That evening...

Isabella, Genevieve, and Beatrice relaxed in the parlour before dinner, the sunlight filtering through the tall windows casting the room in a gentle, ambient glow.

"I must say, Lord Worthington's arrival at the picnic gave me a start," Genevieve confessed. "I feared the whole time that he was there that he might reveal the fact that we were at his house last night! Or even worse, tell everyone about the spanking!" She threw her hand in the air. "Did you hear him comment about how I must like reading books? I nearly died!"

Beatrice shook her head. "Even though they'd both promised not to tell anyone that I'd gone against my brother's wishes, I feared that they would still tell him. It was most alarming!"

Isabella raised her eyebrows. "Yet they said nothing of what had actually occurred; thank goodness. I believe Lord Worthington holds a genuine affection for you, Genevieve," Isabella said, "although I'm not certain he has intentions of marriage."

Genevieve clasped her hands together on her lap. "I find him very exciting and would marry him if he offered. But maybe he's just toying with me—a new plaything, perhaps?"

Beatrice shuddered. "Lord Stansfield quite unnerves me. His eyes were... unsettling. Almost evil."

Isabella took her hand in hers and patted it affectionately. "Erase him from your mind and put what happened down to experience. I have a feeling he won't reveal what happened. His reputation would be at risk, as would yours. You're safe now, Beatrice. And I believe the captain's attention will deter Lord Stansfield."

Beatrice's eyes lit up. "Do you think Captain Harmon likes me?"

Isabella smiled. "Oh, yes, indeed. I think it was quite obvious."

"I noticed it too," Genevieve said, smiling, and then turning to Isabella, she said, "Speaking of attachments, we simply must congratulate you and Lord Somerset! You do make a striking pair."

Beatrice nodded in agreement. "I've never seen my brother so happy. You'll be a wonderful sister to have, Isabella."

As the girls embraced warmly, Isabella glowed with joy. Though doubts lingered, in each other they found true companionship, and she knew they would be there for each other when needed. It was a very comforting thought.

That evening, Lord Somerset kept a watchful eye on Beatrice over dinner. Once Isabella and Genevieve were engaged in a quiet conversation, he turned to his sister.

"Beatrice, I notice Lord Stansfield seemed quite taken with you this afternoon. How do you find him?" he enquired, looking at her intently to see any subtle changes in her expression.

Beatrice shifted in her seat, not meeting his gaze. "He is... intimidating. Far too forward for my liking, if I'm honest."

Lord Somerset nodded knowingly. "I suspected as much. You seemed ill at ease in his presence." A thought occurred. "What of Captain Harmon? I thought you two seemed to get along favourably well until Lord Stansfield arrived."

At the mention of the dashing young soldier, Beatrice's cheeks flushed rosy red, and she confessed softly, "I really like him. The captain is a true gentleman, and speaking to him came so easily."

Lord Somerset smiled, relieved. But he vowed to keep Beatrice from Lord Stansfield's clutches. He wouldn't trust him as far as he could throw him!

"Well then, perhaps we should invite the Captain to join us for dinner one evening?" He suggested.

Beatrice's eyes lit up happily. "That would be lovely!"

Her obvious delight heartened him, and he was truly thankful that she hadn't fallen for Lord Stansfield's dubious interest in her. Reaching for his glass, he sipped the fine vintage and breathed a sigh of relief.

After dinner and with the evening still warm, Lord Somerset offered Isabella his arm to stroll towards the secluded rose gardens. They walked in a comfortable silence for some time, enjoying each other's company.

After a while, he turned to Isabella with concern in his eyes. "Forgive me for prying, but I noticed your worried looks this afternoon when Lord Worthington and Lord Stansfield arrived. Is there anything that I should know?"

Isabella paused, knowing that she couldn't reveal her true qualms about the two men but had to tell him something. "In all truth, I find Lord Stansfield a bit crass, and he seemed to monopolise your sister. I find him rather intimidating. As for Lord Worthington, he's very similar, although Genevieve seems to like him. I wish she didn't, but she has already told me how she feels."

Lord Somerset nodded thoughtfully. "I'd suspected as much. Beatrice has informed me that she has no feelings towards Lord Stansfield and is, in fact, quite enamoured of Captain Harmon."

"She said as much to me earlier. It would be a wonderful match!" Isabella said, genuinely thrilled.

Lord Somerset smiled down at her. "You worry about your friends, don't you? An admirable quality, my love." He squeezed her hand reassuringly. "Have no fear; I'll watch over them too. Together, we'll make sure that nothing untoward happens."

Isabella smiled; her heart warmed at his words, and it gave her some relief. Genevieve was headstrong, and her desire for someone such as Lord Worthington was very worrying. At least with Lord Somerset keeping an eye on her, it may caution her to be a little less hasty.

Reaching a large stone bench, they both sat down and taking her hands, Lord Somerset gazed down at her, his eyes dark and intense. He was so handsome. Her heart fluttered as he reached out, cupped her face with his hand, and touched his lips to hers.

She sighed softly and melted into his kiss, her body responding to him almost of its own will. His tongue meshed with hers, and she felt a jolt of desire shoot through her straight down to the secret place between her thighs. She laid her hand against his chest, feeling the need to touch his virile body. She reveled in the feel of his solid muscles beneath her fingertips, below the fabric of his shirt.

A moment later, they broke apart, slightly breathless, looking at each other with a deep-set emotion.

"My dearest Isabella," he said. "You're so beautiful," he murmured, leaning close. Tenderly, he kissed her lips again.

When he pulled away, Isabella gave a soft sigh of contentment.

Hand in hand, they made their way back to the manor as dusk fell. Pausing on the veranda, Lord Somerset pressed another kiss to Isabella's knuckles. "Sweet dreams, my love. I shall see you tomorrow."

With a final loving glance, Isabella took her leave and headed to her bedroom to dream about the man she loved.

The next evening, there was a grand ball at the Assembly Rooms. Lord Somerset escorted Isabella, Genevieve, and Beatrice safely from their carriage, through the throng of people, and up the wide steps towards the entrance. The grand hall buzzed with the murmur of conversation, the rustle of silk gowns, and the lilting strains of a string quartet.

Guiding the women inside and with a practiced eye, Lord Somerset quickly located a table for them, situated near the dance floor yet offering a degree of privacy. He excused himself, promising to return with refreshments.

Genevieve, her heart aflutter with anticipation, scanned the room for Lord Worthington. A thrill of excitement coursed through her when she spotted him in the corner, engaged in a game of cards with Lord Stansfield. He looked as handsome as ever, his dark hair neatly combed and his piercing blue eyes sparkling with amusement.

Isabella, noticing Genevieve's eagerness, urged caution, "Please be careful, Genevieve. I know you like him, but..."

"Oh, stop worrying, Isabella. I know what I'm doing."

Lord Worthington, sensing their presence, looked up from his cards and met Gevenieve's gaze. A flicker of recognition crossed his face, followed by a calculating smile.

Genevieve returned his smile, her eyes sparkling coquettishly. Isabella couldn't help the shudder that ripped through her. If only her friend wasn't so enamoured of him.

Across the way, Beatrice had already spied the dashing Captain Harmon, who caught her eye and bowed with a smile. She blushed happily and returned his smile shyly.

Lord Somerset returned with a waiter, carrying several drinks, and instructed him to place them on the table.

"I took the liberty of ordering both champagne and punch." He declared, taking a seat. "And there's an excellent buffet if you get hungry later."

"Oh, how lovely!" Isabella said, reaching for a glass of the fruity, peach-coloured punch.

A few moments later, Captain Harmon arrived to ask Beatrice if she would dance with him, to which she readily agreed. As she was whisked away, Isabella couldn't help the smile that broke out on her face. "They make a handsome couple, don't they?"

"Absolutely," Genevieve agreed. Isabella saw her glance over at Lord Worthington again, and very soon he was at their table.

"Lady Genevieve, would you do me the honour of dancing with me?" he declared.

"Of course, I should be delighted," she replied, a smile forming on her lips.

Isabella watched the pair disappear into the crowd and worried her lip with her small teeth. If only Genevieve could like someone else and not a man whose desires were less than suitable.

Lord Somerset reached out and took her hand. "Would you care to dance with me, my love?"

His demand immediately lifted her spirits. She grinned, thankful to have something to take her mind off her friend.

She took to the dance floor, and the pair became lost in their own world as the orchestra played a waltz, Isabella's favourite dance.

Lord Stansfield had been eyeing Beatrice eagerly from across the room. She was perfection. He'd hardly been able to think straight since their last encounter. Her denial to comply with his demands hadn't stopped him for one moment thinking about her peachy little bottom draped over his lap. He just had to find a way for it to happen. His loins stirred at the memory. How he would love to sink his cock deep into her ripe body.

But a frown had marred his brow when he'd noticed the amiable Captain Harmon appear by her side. He couldn't help but notice the way Beatrice's face lit up as he greeted her. His eyes darkened with anger. If that little upstart thought he was going to take away his plaything, then he could think again!

He sipped his brandy and silently decided on his best course of action.

Beatrice had just finished a satisfying twirl around the dance floor with Captain Harmon, and her face was flushed with excitement and exertion. He left her at the side of the room to catch her breath while he went in search of a drink for both of them.

She placed her hand on her chest, feeling her heart racing, not only from the dance but from being in such close proximity to the handsome captain.

"You dance most beautifully, Lady Beatrice," a voice said next to her.

She turned her head to find Lord Stansfield by her side. His eyes glittered with menace, and she immediately took a step backwards.

Seeing her intention, he grabbed her elbow. "Going so soon, my dear?"

She swallowed hard and tried to extricate herself, but his grip was too tight. "I fear you wouldn't like me to make a scene, would you?"

She shook her head.

"Well, then, you will remain and hear what I have to say." He dropped his grip on her elbow and took a sip of his drink before replying, his voice silky smooth but dangerous. "I want you to come to Linden Hall tomorrow night. I will send you an invitation, which you must accept."

"But I don't wish to come." Beatrice whispered.

"You have no choice, because if you don't, then I will have to reveal your indiscretion the last time we met."

Beatrice swallowed hard. "I didn't do anything!"

"You came to Linden Hall against the wishes of your brother, did you not?"

"Yes, but you said you would keep it secret!"

He shot her a cunning smile and said, "Not only that, but you were caught snooping. I think you won't want anyone to know about either. Am I correct?"

"But you can't do that."

"I can. And I will." His smile was evil. "I leave it to you to decide."

He inclined his head and disappeared back into the throng of people, leaving Beatrice as white as a sheet and wondering how she was going to deal with his threat.

Captain Harmon reappeared with a drink for them both and immediately noticed her palour. "Are you unwell, Lady Beatrice? Would you like to step outside and take some fresh air?"

"Thank you; I would." Beatrice replied, eager to move away from the intense atmosphere she had recently found herself in.

Offering her his arm, he led her through the hall and outside into the gardens at the back of the assembly rooms. It was still quite light, and the air was warm with a welcome summer breeze.

"It was a little stuffy inside," she declared, trying to cover up for her appearance.

"You're quite right. I do like to dance, but my heart yearns for the outdoors. Do you like walking, Lady Beatrice?"

"Oh, yes! And riding."

"Perhaps we could take a ride out together this week, if you're available?"

"I should like that very much."

They continued talking, their conversation easy and light. Beatrice pushed all thoughts of Lord Stansfield to the back of her mind for now. She would tell Genevieve and Isabella tonight when she got home, in the hope that they'd be able to help.

Later that night, when everyone had retired for bed, Beatrice crept into Isabella's room and told her what had happened.

"Oh, my, Beatrice. I knew nothing good would come of that dreadful night." Isabella whispered, her eyes wide with shock.

"But what can I do about it? If anyone finds out, it would ruin my family's name, and as for my reputation, it would be in shreds! Captain Harmon would want nothing to do with me!" Her voice ended on a sob, and Isabella quickly put her arms around her.

"Look, we'll find a way to thwart his plans. I don't know how yet, but we will."

"Do you think we should tell Genevieve?"

"She's so infatuated with Lord Worthington that she may not see a solution to your predicament without it impacting on her own relationship." Isabella frowned. "Although, I'm not certain she even has a relationship."

"If I tell my brother, he'll be so angry and disappointed in me. I don't think I could face that."

"Don't worry. Hopefully, it won't come to that. Go to bed and rest. I'll think of something."

When Beatrice had retired to her own bedroom, Isabella lay awake worrying about her friend's predicament. What on earth could she do to help her?

Lord Stansfield was a nasty piece of work, and although she'd told Beatrice that she'd help, she had no idea what to do? If she confronted him herself, he'd most probably just laugh at her.

A man like him couldn't be allowed to threaten people, where was his gentlemanly code of honour? Isabella snorted softly and thumped her pillow. Men like him had no honour!

A vision of Lord Somerset came into her mind. Could she tell him? Should she tell him? She closed her eyes and sighed heavily. She wanted no secrets between them, but this was not about her. It was about his sister.

Groaning, she placed her hands over her face, wondering what on earth she was going to do!

Chapter 6

The next morning, at breakfast, Beatrice was handed a letter by the butler. She stared at it as though it were a coiled snake waiting to strike.

"Aren't you going to open it, my dear?" Lord Somerset queried.

Isabella watched Beatrice's face as she tried to cover up her initial reaction. "Of course. I wonder who it's from." She darted a glance at Isabella, who smiled nervously in response.

Breaking the seal, she unfolded the cream paper and read the contents. Isabella could see she was doing her best to remain calm, but Lord Somerset was watching her intently, and Isabella could tell he knew something wasn't quite right.

"Who is it from, Beatrice?" Genevieve asked, her eyes alight with interest.

"It's an invitation from Lord Stansfield for you and I to attend Linden Hall tomorrow night."

Genevieve gasped, "Oh my! How wonderful!"

Lord Somerset held his hand up in the air, catching her attention. "I maintain my previous decision in that I forbid Beatrice to go, and in all truth, I'm not certain I like the idea of you going alone to the hall, Lady Genevieve." Lord Somerset said.

"Oh, but...!" Genevieve started to say, but Lord Somerset interrupted her.

"You are under my supervision at the moment, and I would feel much happier if you invited Lord Worthington here instead." He glanced at his sister and asked, "Should you like the invitation extended to include Lord Stansfield, my dear, or perhaps Captain Harmon?" He frowned. "Are you quite well, Beatrice?"

Beatrice looked quite pale. "Yes, thank you. I just feel a little lightheaded, that's all."

Isabella watched different emotions cross Genevieve's face. One minute she had looked indignant at being denied an occasion to see Lord Worthington, but then her expression had immediately changed when she realised he could visit Thornfield instead.

"I think the thought of seeing the handsome captain is making you feel so, Beatrice! But don't you think it's a wonderful idea?" Genevieve said excitedly.

"I should like that very much." Beatrice said, "But don't you think Lord Stansfield will be angry at being left out?"

Lord Somerset raised an eyebrow. "It happens to the best of men. Just send him a reply thanking him for his invitation, but you have a prior engagement. Then invite the other two men to dine with us tomorrow night."

Beatrice's colour started to come back, and her cheeks had a rosy flush. "Then I shall go and pen a letter now to both him and Captain Harmon."

"I shall join you! I need to send a note to Lord Worthington. Oh, this will be fun!"

When they'd left, Isabella chewed on a piece of toast, deep in thought. Lord Stansfield was not going to take kindly to her refusal. What if he carried out his threat? Oh lord!

"What is troubling you, my dear?" Lord Somerset asked her, interrupting her thoughts.

Her eyes met his, and she flushed. "Oh, I was just thinking about tomorrow night and what to wear. I have a small hole in my favourite dress."

He narrowed his eyes a little, studying her face. "Are you certain that's the only thing worrying you?"

She nodded quickly. "Of course."

"Very well. I shall send Violet up to your room this afternoon. She has excellent sewing skills."

"Thank you." She fidgeted nervously. Now she would have to make a tiny hole in her dress so the maid wouldn't find anything amiss. "If you'll excuse me, I'll join the other two. Are we still going for a ride this afternoon?"

He nodded and smiled. "Yes, I'm looking forward to it."

When she'd left the room, Lord Somerset pondered to himself. Something wasn't right, and if he was correct, it all revolved around the scheming Lord Stansfield: the way his sister had reacted, the way Isabella had changed expression. He didn't like the man at all, his gut instinct telling him he was a manipulative rogue.

But it went deeper than that. Did he have some sort of hold over the girls that they weren't telling him?

He made a note to talk to Isabella later in the afternoon, when they were alone. He would take her in his arms and kiss her soundly until she revealed everything. The thought of her soft lips pressed against his made him ache with a deep set desire. The sooner he could make her his bride, the better.

After lunch and under a beautiful, clear blue sky, Lord Somerset joined Isabella for a horse ride upon the picturesque rolling hills that stretched just beyond the boundaries of his estate. It was a chance for them to be alone, and in all truth, he had thought of nothing but kissing her since breakfast!

As they cantered along the winding paths, the wind tousling their hair, he couldn't help but admire the way she rode. She was a natural and controlled the small mare with ease and poise. Her hair, which had been neatly pinned, was now coming loose, with small tendrils falling about her heart-shaped face. Her cheeks were flushed from the fresh air, and she looked more beautiful than ever.

He urged his horse faster, his eagerness to feel the softness of her lips against his own of utmost urgency. But there was another pressing matter that weighed heavily on his mind: the secret that Lord Stansfield held over his sister, Lady Beatrice.

One way or another, he would find out the truth.

As the horses slowed to a gentle trot, Isabella glanced over at Lord Somerset. He smiled and guided his horse closer to hers, his eyes searching hers.

"You ride very well, my lord," she grinned. "Almost as well as I do!"

"Impudent miss!" he laughed, showing his even white teeth.

She loved to hear him laugh. He looked even more handsome if that were possible.

"Come, we'll sit down over there, overlooking the hill, and then I can kiss you." he stated, his eyes darkening with a deep hunger.

She flushed becomingly, her breath catching in her throat as a deep wave of desire washed over her.

Tethering their horses, he took a seat on the ground and patted the grass. She sat down, and he immediately placed one of his strong arms around her, drawing her straight onto his lap. She sighed submissively when his lips claimed hers, her small hands sliding up to his shoulders and entwining at the back of his neck. He deepened the kiss, his tongue seeking entrance into her soft warmth. She opened for him without hesitation. It felt heavenly.

She felt his hand on her breast, his thumb gently grazing over the stiffened nipple. His tongue entwining with hers was driving her crazy with desire, her body becoming heated and pliable.

His mouth left hers, and he trailed a line of kisses down her arched neck, down to the swell of her bosom.

When his lips pressed against her alabaster skin, she almost swooned. She sighed throatily, but made no move to stop him.

Lord Somerset raised his head slightly and took in her flushed appearance. The desire to take things further was an urge he had to fight hard to control. He could feel his loins tighten, and it took all his willpower to overcome the primal need to seek release.

She opened her eyes and stared back at him softly, her lips pouting and swollen from his kisses.

"You're so beautiful." He said, his gaze roving over her flushed face.

She smiled and played with the hair at the nape of his neck, where her hands were still entwined. She felt good in his arms. She fitted perfectly.

"Will you marry me, Isabella? I think we know we're both suited by now, and I don't want to wait any longer to have you as my wife."

"Oh!"

He watched the play of emotions cross her face. "Are you surprised?"

"A little. I had thought you'd want to court a little longer, but in all truth, I feel just the same. I would be honoured to become your wife." Her eyes sparkled back at him.

He kissed her soundly, leaving her breathless. "Then I will move heaven and earth to get it done forthwith! The sooner you're mine, the better. Do you think your parents will have any objections?"

"Oh, no, not at all." She said, smiling.

"Then we shall ride over to visit with them in the next few days, and I will ask your father's permission. It's only a thirty-minute or so ride by carriage from here to Walliswood. I'm quite looking forward to meeting them."

She leaned her head against his chest, still curled up on his lap. He kissed the top of her head gently before asking, "Isabella, there's something I need to know," he began, his tone filled with concern. "I'm troubled by Lord Stansfield."

He felt Isabella's body tense. It was only slight, but he knew instantly that his assumptions were correct. Something was going on.

He continued, keeping his tone light so as not to intimidate her. He wanted the truth and would gently pry it from her. "Does he have a hold over my sister? Has something happened between them that I don't know about?"

Isabella's eyes widened slightly as she listened intently to Lord Somerset's question.

She took a moment to collect her thoughts, her gaze lowered so he couldn't see her expression.

Should she tell him the truth? She understood the gravity of the situation and the importance of revealing the secret liaison that had led to Beatrice's predicament, but what if Lord Somerset blamed his sister for what had happened? What if he punished her or banished her from their estate?

She took a deep breath, and with a resolute expression, she looked up at him, her voice steady yet filled with empathy.

"If I tell you something, will you promise not to be angry?"

Lord Somerset put his hand on her chin and looked deep into her eyes. "I cannot promise, but I think you must tell me what has occurred."

In a small voice, Isabella revealed to him the circumstances that had led to Lord Stansfield thinking he could blackmail Beatrice to do his bidding. It was a dangerous game of manipulation and deceit, fueled by the risqué books that all three of them had dared to discover. She refrained from telling him that she still secretly possessed one of them. That was a step too far.

"So you see," she continued tentatively, "Genevieve seems quite content to receive Lord Worthington's attention, whereas your sister has regretted what happened ever since. I must tell you that both Genevieve and Beatrice were quite intoxicated at the time. I know it doesn't alter what happened, but I feel, given that they were both not in their right states of mind, that they should be forgiven for any misdeeds." She plucked nervously at her skirts. "It's Lord Stansfield who has threatened to expose your sister's secret and tarnish your family name if she doesn't comply with his demands. He is a scoundrel!"

Lord Somerset's face had turned dark with anger, and she watched in fascination as his jaw tightened.

Lord Somerset's heart sank at the confirmation of his suspicions, yet a flicker of determination ignited within him. He knew that he couldn't allow Lord Stansfield to continue his manipulations unchecked. His sister's well-being and their family's reputation depended on his ability to expose the truth and put an end to the blackmail.

But what about Genevieve? He couldn't allow her to continue in such a fashion. It was one thing for a husband to spank his wife, in fact, it was his duty. To keep one's wife safe from harm if she acted in a willful manner was of utmost importance, and if she needed a reminder on how to behave, it was fitting for her husband to chastise her.

But for Lord Worthington to do such a thing to Genevieve, who was in no way attached to him, was most indecent and didn't speak well of his character. Not at all. It was a side of his nature that he'd managed to keep well hidden. And what gave Lord Worthington the idea that he could see his sister, Beatrice, spoken to in such a fashion by Lord Stansfield? The whole affair was abominable.

He paused for a moment and looked into his fiancée's eyes. "I should punish you for daring to snoop around Lord Worthington's house like that. In fact, all three of you should be punished. He had expressly forbidden you to go into that part of the house, yet you all disobeyed him!"

She had the temerity to look ashamed and hung her head a little, her bottom lip pouting.

"You should know by now that prying only leads to trouble. If I ever find out you've done anything like this again, I will put you straight over my knee. Do you understand?"

She nodded and looked at him from beneath her lashes, her heart beating furiously.

"But it was commendable of you to tell me the truth. I just have to find a solution now."

With renewed resolve, he lifted her gently off his lap and stood up. They reclaimed their mounts and continued their ride home, both of them deep in thought. Isabella wondering if she'd done the right thing and Lord Somerset thinking of several ways to ruin the despicable Lord Stansfield and how he was going to deal with Lord Worthington when he saw him.

Chapter 7

The next day, Lord Somerset made his way towards Lord Stansfield's estate, his resolve growing stronger with each passing moment. The weight of his family's honour rested upon his shoulders, and he was determined to put an end to the malicious games that threatened to tarnish their name.

He still couldn't believe his sister had dared to get involved with such a cad. He'd never liked him from the onset, and Isabella's revelation had only proved his initial reservations to be correct.

Beatrice had been mortified when he'd confronted her about her initial involvement with the rogue and had, after gentle persuasion, finally revealed the whole truth, confirming every word that Isabella had told him. It had ended up in tears, but he'd reassured her that nothing would come of the scoundrel's evil intentions. He would make sure of it.

So here he was, and with every step he took, his determination solidified, fueling his need to confront Lord Stansfield head-on.

As he approached the imposing entrance of Lord Stansfield's house, Lord Somerset's heart pounded with a mix of anticipation and righteous anger. He knew this wasn't going to be easy, but he had no doubt that his words would carry weight. After all, his family's reputation spoke for itself, and he felt confident that he could stop Lord Stansfield's manipulative scheme.

A dour-looking butler opened the door and invited him into a rather grand foyer. Moments later, Lord Stansfield appeared, a nonchalant smile on his face. It was clear that he had not expected Lord Somerset's visit, but he quickly composed himself, masking his surprise.

"Lord Somerset," Lord Stansfield greeted him, his voice dripping with false charm. "What a pleasant surprise. To what do I owe the honour of your visit?"

Lord Somerset's eyes hardened as he met Lord Stansfield's gaze. He had no time for pleasantries, only a direct confrontation that would expose the dishonourable intent that lay beneath the rogue's facade.

"I'm here to address a matter of utmost importance," Lord Somerset replied, his voice firm and resolute. "I know of your attempts to blackmail my sister, Lady Beatrice, and if you think, for one minute, that I'll allow you to exploit her, then you're clearly deluded."

Lord Stansfield's eyes widened in feigned innocence, a well-practiced act that did not sway Lord Somerset's conviction. "Blackmail? I'm afraid you must be mistaken, Lord Somerset. I assure you, I've no idea what you mean!"

Lord Somerset's expression remained unyielding, his voice laced with an undeniable sense of authority. "Don't underestimate me, Lord Stansfield. My family's honour isn't something to be trifled with, and I will protect it at all costs."

A flicker of uncertainty passed across Lord Stansfield's face, his composed demeanor giving way to a hint of concern. He had obviously not anticipated such a direct and forceful confrontation and had hoped to presume upon his sister's youthful innocence.

Lord Somerset leaned in closer, his eyes locked with Lord Stansfield's. "Let this be a warning. You will never darken my house again. Your schemes and manipulations will cease immediately, and should you ever attempt to harm my sister or anyone else, you *will* face the consequences."

With his message delivered, Lord Somerset turned on his heel and strode toward the exit, leaving Lord Stansfield standing in stunned silence. The weight of Lord Somerset's words hung in the air, a clear indication that he would never back down, nor would he allow Lord Stansfield to continue his malicious endeavors.

As Lord Somerset made his way back to his own estate, he felt a sense of satisfaction. He had stood up for his family's honour, confronting the manipulator who sought to tarnish their name. He'd made his position clear, and if Lord Stansfield chose to defy him, then he would truly regret it!

Isabella paced up and down the parlour, wringing her hands together nervously. What if Lord Somerset couldn't get Lord Stansfield to see reason?

Beatrice was standing by the window, staring at the drive, as she waited for her brother to return.

She sighed heavily and turned to look at Isabella.

"My mind is in turmoil. One minute I'm thrilled that Captain Harmon will be coming to dine with us tonight, and the next I'm terrified that my brother will be unable to stop Lord Stansfield's attempt to blackmail me."

Isabella walked over to her and, placing a hand on her shoulder, attempted to comfort her. "Think only positive thoughts, dearest. Your brother is a formidable man, and his authority far exceeds that of Lord Stansfield. I think he will rue the day he attempted to pursue you in such a despicable manner."

"I do hope you're right." She turned back around to look out of the window.

Just then, Genevieve breezed into the room, her face alight with excitement. "Lord Worthington has just replied, saying that he'll be only too honoured to dine with us tonight!" She held his letter aloft. "He has such fine handwriting!"

"I'm happy for you, Genevieve, but at the moment we're a little preoccupied." Isabella said, silently urging her to tone it down a little.

"Oh!" She pulled a face. "I'm sorry! I forgot Lord Somerset was going to see Lord Stansfield this morning."

Isabella had, with Beatrice's permission, told Genevieve about Lord Stansfield's behaviour in the hope that it might dissuade her from seeing Lord Worthington again. But it hadn't. She'd condemned Lord Stansfield but declared that Lord Worthington would never do such a thing. She was so besotted with him, Isabella doubted anything would put her off the man!

Genevieve walked over to stand beside Beatrice and peered out of the window. "Has he been gone long?"

"About an hour." Beatrice worried her bottom lip and then, turning around, walked over to one of the couches and threw herself down into it, her expression weary. "I can't stand the suspense!"

"Well, I don't think you have long to wait now, for your brother is coming up the drive!" Genevieve declared.

All three of them raced out of the room and hurried to the entrance, eager to hear what he had to say.

Isabella watched as Lord Somerset dismounted, admiring his strong features and athletic body. He didn't look too angry; in fact, she would say he looked quite relieved.

Lord Somerset glanced up the outer stone staircase to see the three of them gathered to see him. He smiled and strode quickly up the steps.

"Did you get to speak with him?" Beatrice asked, clasping her hands together in worry. "What did he say?"

"Come inside, and we shall discuss it quietly in the parlour."

Standing before them a few moments later and with a resolute expression, Lord Somerset began to speak, his voice carrying a mix of determination and reassurance.

"I confronted Lord Stansfield regarding his attempts to blackmail you, Beatrice. I made it abundantly clear that such actions would not be tolerated, and I believe I have successfully put an end to his malicious intentions."

Beatrice's eyes widened, a mix of relief and gratitude washing over her features. "Oh, thank goodness!"

Isabella and Genevieve exchanged glances, their expressions reflecting Beatrice's.

Lord Somerset continued, "At first, he tried to deny the accusations, but with a little persuasion, he realised it was futile. I've warned him to stay away from you, Beatrice, and to cease any attempt to tarnish our family's name." His voice was firm and resolute. "I made it clear that any further slander or ill-intentions towards you will not go unanswered. The law will be on our side, and I'll not hesitate to protect the honour of our family through legal means if necessary."

Beatrice's relief was clear to see. She rushed over and hugged him gratefully. "I've always known you to be a man of honour and integrity, brother. I don't know what I'd do without you."

"I think keeping away from men like Lord Stansfield would be a good start, my dear." He looked down at her meaningfully, and she had the grace to look ashamed.

With the tension gone, everyone started to relax. Isabella had never been more certain that marrying Lord Somerset was the right thing to do.

That afternoon

Isabella was lazing under a large oak tree alone, lying on a blanket and keeping out of the glare of the midday sun. Genevieve and Beatrice had opted to go into town to visit the boutiques but Isabella preferred some time alone with her book. The last few days had been hectic and a little respite was most welcome.

She turned the page and suddenly sensed someone nearby. She glanced up to find Lord Somerset standing next to her. She hadn't heard him approach, for the soft grass had absorbed the sound of his footsteps.

She went to smile and then saw his expression. He was angry. Very angry. She looked down at his hand and noticed he was holding something, and her eyes widened in dismay when she realised what it was—the stolen book!

She sat up quickly, her heart hammering in her chest. How on earth he had got hold of it, she had no idea, but judging by his stormy expression, he was far from happy.

Oh, lord!

"This was found in your bedroom. Would you care to explain?"

Isabella gulped.

"I know it doesn't belong to me," he continued, "and certainly wouldn't be in my collection. I can only assume you brought it with you!"

Caught off guard, Isabella's mind raced. What could she say? It was Genevieve who had persuaded her to bring the damn thing. She truly wished she had burned the blasted book!

In a moment of desperation, she chose to lie. "I have no idea what it's doing in my room. Honestly, I don't!"

Lord Somerset, however, was not easily fooled. "You're lying."

Isabella raised her chin and said, "I'm not!"

He hunkered down beside her, placing a hand under her chin. "Don't lie to me. It's most unbecoming. Now, tell me the truth. Where did you get such a risqué book, or do I even need to ask?"

She realised she had to say something, so she blurted out, "Oh, I... err... found it in the stables!" she said in a rush.

"And I'm expected to believe that, am I? Do you take me for a fool, Isabella?"

Isabella squirmed uncomfortably and realised she was going to have to tell the truth, or part thereof. "I stole it."

He stood back up, and his eyes darkened. "Stole it?"

She gulped and revealed she'd taken it from Lord Worthington's library.

"I'm disappointed in you, Isabella. Firstly, you don't steal, and secondly, what on earth were you doing keeping a book like this? Have you no regard for your reputation?"

Isabella recoiled under his obvious fury and sat silently while he scolded her for her dishonesty and for keeping secrets from him.

He looked at her, his expression grim. "I've got a good mind to send you home right this minute, but I care for you too much, so I'm going to give you a lesson that you won't forget."

"What do you mean?" Isabella could hardly breathe. What was he going to do?

Isabella scrambled to her feet and looked at him askance. Was he going to call off the engagement? Was he going to banish her?

He took hold of her arm and drew her near to him. "My dearest Isabella, I love you so much, but I will not tolerate lying or putting yourself in danger, so I'm going to spank your bottom so you don't forget this moment, and it will ensure that you never, ever do anything like this again!"

She tried to pull away from him. "Spank me? But you can't do that!"

"Do you remember the conversation we had the other day when I said you should be punished? I told you that if you put yourself in trouble or in harm's way, then I would have no hesitation in putting you over my knee."

Her face flushed beet red, and she looked down at the ground. Oh yes, she remembered alright.

"Now, you will follow me." He said firmly.

Isabella thought about running, but where would she go? And she knew, deep down, that she should never have taken that book. Oh, Lord, now she was in for it!

She put her arm through his as he led her across the lawns and up the stairs into the house. Before long, they were standing outside his study. He opened the thick wooden door and ushered her inside the wood-paneled room. The smell of leather-bound books and the faint hint of woodsmoke assailed her senses, and ordinarily, she would have found it comforting. Today, however, it was anything but.

He led her over to his desk and pulled out a chair, which he swiftly sat down on. She gulped as she took in his stern demeanour and knew that what she was about to receive was going to be painful.

He pulled her down over his lap and moved her forward, so her toes were barely touching the ground. She closed her eyes with embarrassment.

"You are one reckless little madam; do you know that?" He swiftly pulled up her skirts until her bloomers were exposed. These he quickly unlaced, tugging them down to her knees so her bottom was fully exposed to his appreciative gaze.

Isabella felt the cool air on her bottom and closed her eyes even tighter, mortified. How on earth was she in this position? All over one book!

She thought about resisting and attempted to struggle, but his grip was too strong, and he gave her a sharp spank in return. "Desist, Isabella! You know by now that I'm a man of my word. And you, my girl, are in for a very red bottom!"

"Oh, upon my word! You cannot treat me like this; let me up!" She rebelled and tried to wriggle out of her punishment, but Lord Somerset was far too strong.

"No!" He said, tightening his grip around her waist, "You need to be taught a lesson on how to behave!" His hand descended onto both cheeks at once, making them wobble with the impact. He followed with several spanks in quick succession, quickly turning the creamy flesh into a dark pink hue.

Isabella cried out, struggling to no avail. Her bottom was really beginning to hurt, and she just wanted it to stop.

Lord Somerset, however, had other plans. His hands made light work of his task; in fact, he was thoroughly enjoying himself. The sight of her beautiful, peachy little bottom laid out before him was something to behold. Anyway, she only had herself to blame for being in this position.

He had warned her, and she had thought to ignore him. She would learn to behave if it was the last thing he did!

He brought his hand down fast and hard, with no let up in between.

Her bottom jiggled under the onslaught, and it brought pleasure to his eyes. She would soon learn that her intended husband wasn't a man to be trifled with.

Her small cries filled the room, but he didn't stop; he intended for her to remember this punishment and perhaps deter her from future mischief! Finally, after another few smacks, he brought her punishment to a close.

His hand rested on her warm, pert cheeks while he admired their perfect curve. He began to softly stroke them while speaking, "You, Miss, have a lot to learn. Don't ever lie to me and certainly never steal, do you hear?"

He couldn't help but notice a drip of moisture between her legs, and the desire to touch her in that most sacred of places overcame his sense of propriety. Before he could control his thoughts, his finger slipped between her supple folds. He heard her sharp intake of breath, but she made no move to stop him.

Gently, he rubbed the slippery flesh, revelling in the fact that she seemed to be as aroused as he was. Finding her small nub of desire, he began a gentle rubbing, listening and reacting to her soft cries of desire. When, a few short moments later, her whole body tensed and she gave a small gasp, he knew she had reached her climax.

He removed his hand and rubbed her rosy-red bottom before pulling her up to sit on his lap. She looked at him, her eyes soft and dewy, her lips parted slightly, and he instantly captured her lips with his own. Grazing her soft flesh and demanding a response, which she willingly gave.

Breaking away, he murmured against her mouth. "We will visit your parents tomorrow, and then I will arrange for us to get married by special licence; I cannot wait much longer."

Isabella's mind was in turmoil, her heart was all aflutter. One minute she felt anger towards him for treating her thus, but on the other hand, she found herself responding to his authority, plus his ministrations had just given her more pleasure than she'd ever known!

As for getting married soon, well, truth to tell, she couldn't wait either. She smiled, her eyes staring dreamily into his, and said, "Then we must hurry and organise our wedding, for when I become your wife, it will be the happiest day of my life."

His eyes darkened with desire, and she found herself lost once again as his lips devoured hers, leaving her in no doubt of his intentions towards her.

Chapter 8

That evening

Isabella took her place at the dining table and shifted uncomfortably. Something that Lord Somerset noticed immediately. When her eyes flashed to his with a small look of defiance, he raised an eyebrow in warning so she quickly looked away. She only had herself to blame for having a sore bottom and hopefully she would learn from it.

As the dinner progressed, Lord Somerset observed the interactions between his guests with a keen eye. Lord Worthington's attentiveness towards Lady Genevieve didn't go unnoticed. It was evident that he admired her, but did his intention lend itself to making an honest woman of her?

As he watched them engage in conversation, a glimmer of hope sparked within him. Perhaps, just perhaps, he had actually fallen in love with her. As for his rather unusual book collection and the way he'd treated her that night, it was something he was going to have to talk to him about.

On the other side of the table, Captain Harmon was charming and quite devoted to his sister. Lord Somerset watched his eyes sparkle with genuine interest, as if every word that Beatrice spoke held immeasurable value. It was clear that a connection was forming, one that had the potential to blossom into something beautiful. He hoped so, for his sister deserved such an eligible husband.

Amidst the warm atmosphere, Lord Somerset couldn't help but steal glances at his soon-to-be wife, Isabella. Her innocent beauty and lively conversation made him smile. She was the ideal woman to grace Thornfield, and for him, she was the perfect match.

The evening continued amiably, and when the time came for his guests to depart, Lord Somerset asked if Lord Worthington would join him in the study for a moment so they could speak privately. He agreed, and once Captain Harmon had departed and the women had retired, Lord Somerset showed him into the sanctity of his study.

With a sombre expression, Lord Somerset got straight to the point. "You and I have been friends for a long time, but I have recently become aware of something that gives me cause for concern."

"Oh?"

"I know what occurred the other night at your house involving not only my sister but Lady Genevieve, and I find I'm deeply disappointed in your actions towards both of them."

Lord Worthington's eyes widened in surprise, a mixture of guilt and defiance creeping into his features. "I see, but what business is it of yours? They are both adults."

"They are young adults, both innocent of the world's affairs. I care very much for Lady Genevieve and her family. As for my sister, my regard for her is beyond measure." He gave him a hard stare. "A woman's reputation is a fine thing, and what you did was scandalous beyond words."

"Nothing happened to your sister, and Lady Genevieve was a willing participant." He said, tight-lipped.

"The fact that you allowed my sister to be treated like that is quite unforgivable. How on earth did you meet such a man as Lord Stansfield?"

"Through my business dealings in London. We found we have similar tastes."

"I believe you would be wise to part company with such a man. Did he tell you that he tried to blackmail my sister?"

Lord Worthington looked quite shocked. "No, I had no idea! When did this happen?"

"Two days ago, at the ball in the Assembly Rooms." Lord Somerset looked at him accusingly and asked, "Is this the sort of man you wish to be associated with?"

Lord Worthington sat down on a nearby chair and rubbed a hand over his chin, his face troubled. "I had no idea he would stoop so low."

"As for Lady Genevieve, even if she was willing, it's certainly not how a gentleman treats a lady. Unless, of course, your intention is to marry her?"

He raised an eyebrow and asked, "Would you make me?"

"Yes, in a heartbeat, but only if this incident becomes known. At the moment, it hasn't come to that, but continue and see what happens."

Lord Worthington sighed and rubbed his forehead. "I suppose it was foolish and careless of me."

Lord Somerset's gaze hardened as he continued, his voice firm and unwavering. "Foolish indeed, but your actions have consequences. I will not stand by and allow such behaviour to continue. Lady Genevieve deserves better, and I will not let her be treated as a mere plaything."

Lord Worthington's expression faltered as he realized the gravity of the situation. He'd never expected his actions to be discovered, nor the repercussions that would follow. He knew he'd made a grave mistake, one that he could no longer ignore.

Lord Somerset took a moment to collect his thoughts, his gaze fixed on Lord Worthington. "I watched you two tonight, and I can see a genuine attraction between you. Do you love her?"

Lord Worthington's expression softened, a flicker of genuine emotion crossing his face. "Yes, I suppose I do. It was never my intention to hurt her, but I found myself unable to resist the pull of our connection. I felt it the moment I set eyes on her."

Lord Somerset sighed, his stance softening slightly. "While I cannot condone your previous actions, I'm quite willing to forget what I've been told on one condition - I think you should strongly think about marrying her."

Lord Worthington nodded solemnly, seeming to understand the weight of Lord Somerset's words. "I confess, I find her enchanting. I will marry Lady Genevieve if she'll have me and make amends for any pain I have caused."

Lord Somerset's expression softened, "Very well. I trust that you will honour your commitment."

"I will call again tomorrow and propose to her. You have my word."

With their conversation concluded, Lord Somerset watched Lord Worthington leave on his thoroughbred horse, his troubled mind eased by their conversation. He just hoped he would keep to his word.

The next day, Lord Worthington arrived at Thornfield and invited Genevieve to walk with him in the gardens. Beatrice and Isabella sat in the parlour giving them time alone.

Beatrice was making an effort at embroidery, and Isabella was trying to read a book, but neither of them could focus properly.

"Do you think he'll propose?" Beatrice asked her, her needle poised.

"He did seem very attentive to her last night. I do hope so, for she's very much in love with him."

Although Isabella didn't care for Lord Worthington's rather questionable library, she did realise that with his wealth, he'd be able to give Genevieve a life of luxury that she was already accustomed to. Genevieve had made it clear that she was deeply in love with him, and how they chose to spend their private moments was, of course, their concern.

And after being chastised herself by Lord Somerset, she could see the thin line between pleasure and pain. Her heart fluttered at the thought of being put in such a position again, and she felt her cheeks begin to blush.

Pushing the thought from her mind, she tried again to focus on the book in front of her. But it was hard.

A little while later, the parlour door was thrown open, and Genevieve rushed in like a whirlwind.

"Oh, my! I am to become Lady Worthington! Can you imagine?"

Isabella jumped up. "Truly?"

"Oh, I cannot believe it!" She grinned, "But it's true. Lord Worthington just proposed this very minute."

"Has he left already?" Beatrice asked. "We haven't even had time to congratulate him."

"Yes, he has urgent business in town, but he has promised to return tomorrow so we can begin to discuss our wedding plans." She turned to Isabella. "What news, Isabella! Both you and I are engaged to be married. Who would have believed our summer would work out so well?"

Isabella smiled. Genevieve's exuberance was always a joy, and it gave her warmth in her heart to see her so happy. She just hoped that Lord Worthington would prove himself to be the husband she so desired.

"No, indeed, it has been a most eventful summer, yet it's still not over." Isabella darted a wicked glance at Beatrice. "Perhaps Captain Harmon will become your suitor, Beatrice? Then all three of us shall be married. What do you say to that?"

Beatrice flushed becomingly. "A pleasant thought indeed, Isabella!"

That afternoon, Isabella and Lord Somerset took the carriage towards Walliswood. He held her hand the whole way and couldn't help but kiss her several times during the journey. By the time they arrived, Isabella felt quite dizzy with excitement.

Her parents were very welcoming to Lord Somerset, as she knew they would be, and when he asked for her hand in marriage, her dear father happily agreed.

Her mother was almost beside herself with joy and talked non-stop about the wedding arrangements and where to procure the best seamstress and the freshest flowers. On and on, she went. So much so that Isabella was thankful to step back into the carriage.

As the wheels of the carriage trundled up the driveway, she leaned back in her seat and smiled at Lord Somerset.

His eyes crinkled with mirth. "I think your mother is very happy with your choice of husband, my love. What say you?"

"Oh, indeed. I have made the wisest of choices."

She leaned forward and pressed her lips against his. It was the only prompting he needed. She soon found herself swept onto his lap, and his mouth claimed hers in a passionate kiss that left her quite breathless and in no doubt of his love and admiration.

The next day, with Lord Worthington ensconced in the study discussing the marriage details with Genevieve, Isabella and Beatrice decided to take a trip into town to visit the boutiques. Lord Somerset had insisted they take the carriage rather than ride on horseback as the weather was threatening rain and he didn't want them to come down with any ailments.

Isabella smiled to herself at his concern. He was such a thoughtful man.

The carriage arrived in the small town of Cranleigh, and both girls alighted, telling the driver that they'd be back in a few hours. Beatrice slipped him a couple of coins so he could have an ale with his friends at the inn.

"You're as thoughtful as your brother, Beatrice." Isabella noted, smiling. "What a family I am marrying into."

They slipped their arms through each other and strolled towards the first boutique, neither seeing the dark figure that slipped down the side of a nearby alley.

Lord Stansfield watched Beatrice from the narrow, shady side alley. She was so beautiful and graceful. His eyes narrowed. If only he could have her for himself.

Her brother's warning had scared him a little, if he was to be honest, but at the same time, his desire for the winsome girl far outweighed any threat. He wasn't used to being denied what he wanted. His wealth could buy anything, usually. Most people had their price, but not in this instance, it would seem.

His mind schemed as his beady eyes followed her every step. When the two girls disappeared inside Madame Blake's boutique, he knew he had to make a move. He might never get another opportunity, not with the honourable Captain Harmon sniffing around her.

With a stealth to his step, he emerged from the alley and began to form a plan.

Standing at the counter, waiting for their purchases to be wrapped, Beatrice said to Isabella, "I'm so hungry! If you finish up here, I'll go and see if there's room in the tea rooms for us. Last time I came, it was so busy we couldn't get a table."

"Oh, Lord! I'm famished too." Isabella replied. "Make haste! I'll meet you there shortly. I just need to choose some ribbon, and I'll be done."

Ten minutes later, and telling Madame Blake to deliver the parcels to their coachman, Isabella set off for the tea rooms just up the main thoroughfare. She walked quickly, her mouth salivating at the thought of a buttered scone with jam and a splendid cup of tea to accompany it.

The doorbell tinkled above her head as she ventured inside. It was busy, but there were still a couple of tables free. Looking around, she couldn't see Beatrice.

Frowning, she asked one of the waitresses if she had seen her. "No, ma'am. Lady Beatrice hasn't been in today, to my knowledge."

"Maybe you didn't notice her? Is there anyone else here that might have seen her come in?"

"I'll go and ask Sarah. She and I are the only two on duty today."

Isabella waited anxiously for her to return, her mind working overtime. The girl returned, her expression a little perplexed. "No, she hasn't seen her either, ma'am."

"Oh, dear!" She wrung her hands together nervously, realising something must have happened. But what? She looked at the waitress and said, "If you do see Lady Beatrice, could you tell her I'm looking for her?"

"Will do, ma'am."

Isabella left the tea room in a bit of a daze, with a feeling of foreboding in her bones. Where on earth was she?

Retracing her steps, she visited Madame Blake's boutique again to see if Beatrice had returned, but there was no sign of her. Feeling quite panicked, Isabella frantically began to scour the town, her eyes darting from one corner to another and her mind racing with fear and desperation. She questioned every passerby, hoping to catch a glimpse of Lady Beatrice or any information that could guide her in her search. But no one could tell her anything. It was as though she had disappeared into thin air!

With a heavy heart, Isabella returned to Thornfield, telling the driver to get her there as soon as was humanly possible. Running up the steps, she quickly sought out Lord Somerset, her voice trembling as she relayed the devastating news of his sister's disappearance.

Lord Somerset's face contorted with a mixture of anguish and shock. "But where could she have gone? Cranleigh is not a big town. Was she well when she left you in the boutique?"

"Very well. She was not poorly at all." She wrung her hands together, hardly believing what had happened.

Lord Somerset's mind was racing. Where could his sister have gone? As worried as he was, he could see how badly it had affected Isabella.

"Come and sit down, my love." He poured her a small glass of brandy. "Sip that; it will calm your nerves. I will send Parkin to bring Genevieve to sit with you. She's in the rose garden at the moment, taking some air. I will leave it to you to tell her what's happened. As for me, I must hurry to town."

He kissed her forehead and quickly left the room. Without a moment's hesitation, he mounted his horse and rode towards Cranleigh, his mind consumed with thoughts of Beatrice's safety and the urgency to bring her back unharmed.

Arriving in town, Lord Somerset wasted no time in questioning the locals, his voice filled with a sense of urgency and desperation. It seemed no one could help until, finally, a man in the corner of the tavern caught his attention. The man was a little bit worse for wear, having imbibed quite a lot of ale by the looks of things but when he raised his finger to catch Lord Somerset's attention, he immediately approached him.

"Do you know of my sister's whereabouts?" He said without preamble. "Did you witness anything that could lead me to her?"

The man hesitated, his eyes darting about the tavern nervously. "I don't like saying nothin' against the gentry, like, my lord, but I can tell yuh with certainty that I saw Lord Stansfield near the stables. He had a dark-haired young woman with him, struggling against his grip. They entered a carriage swiftly and then disappeared up the road."

Lord Somerset's blood turned cold. So Lord Stansfield was involved! The woman the man described had to be his sister. It was too much of a coincidence.

His heart sank, a mixture of anger and determination pulsating through his veins. With newfound clarity, he knew his next course of action. He would pursue Lord Stansfield relentlessly, no matter the cost, until Beatrice was safely returned into his safe keeping.

"Do you know in which direction they went?" He asked the man.

"London way, I'd say."

"You've been most helpful." Lord Somerset said, flicking the man a coin. With time of the essence, he left the tavern and quickly remounted his horse, setting off towards London with one mission. To save his sister from certain ruin.

Chapter 9

The next morning, Isabella awoke and found out that Lord Somerset had still not returned. Anxiously, she joined Genevieve at the breakfast table.

"What is to be done, Isabella?" Genevieve asked, her face full of concern.

"I know not. I just hope and pray Lord Somerset manages to find her."

"Do you think something nefarious has happened to her?"

"I'm afraid it must have. If she'd fallen ill, someone would know. Someone would have called the doctor." She thrummed her fingers on the table in agitation. "But as it is, no one has any news of her at all!"

Genevieve took a small bite of her toast and, chewing thoughtfully, said, "What if she's eloped with Captain Harmon?"

"No! He would never do such a thing. He's far too much of a gentleman!"

"What if she's been abducted? What if Lord Stansfield is involved?"

Isabella closed her eyes in despair. "If so, then I hope with all my heart that Lord Somerset finds them before... Oh, I cannot even say the words!"

"Before she is defiled in the most vile manner." Genevieve added for her.

They looked at each other, their eyes wide and tears slipping down their cheeks.

Lord Somerset had spent most of the evening scouring the streets, asking strangers if they had seen Lord Stansfield or his sister. After several weary hours, he discovered that Lord Stansfield possessed a townhouse nestled within the prestigious Oxford Street. Firmly tapping his cane against the front door, it swung open to reveal a butler who, in a feeble attempt, sought to shut it promptly in Lord Somerset's face. Undeterred by this initial resistance, Lord Somerset's resolve remained unshaken, and with a broad shoulder against the door, he prevented its closure.

"Lord Stansfield, at once!" he declared, his eyes blazing.

The butler quickly disappeared into one of the rooms, but before he could return, Lord Somerset was already shadowing him.

The sight that met his eyes that day would never leave him. His dearest sister was bound to a wooden chair by her ankles and her wrists, her mouth silenced by a silken gag. Her eyes were red and bloodshot from the tears she'd shed. He had never known such fury.

With eyes of steel, he turned to stare at the man who had dared take his most precious sister. Lord Stansfield had been in the midst of writing but now sprang up, his face wild and shocked at the intrusion.

The butler, sensing trouble afoot, quickly backed out of the room.

"What the devil do you think you're playing at?" Lord Somerset said, his eyes dark and foreboding.

Lord Stansfield picked up his sword and brandished it at Lord Somerset. "Stand aside. She is mine now."

"Yours? How dare you!" Lord Somerset spat, his lip curling in anger. "If you have ruined her..."

"Oh, I tried," Lord Stansfield's lip curled back, "but this little madam has too much spunk for my liking, but I can change that given time!"

Lord Somerset saw red, and raising his cane, he brought it straight down against Lord Stansfield's sword. As it fell from his hands, Lord

Stansfield tried to lunge at Lord Somerset to throw him off balance, but Lord Somerset stepped aside, and Lord Stansfield ended up in an untidy sprawl on the floor. Not wasting a moment, Lord Somerset grabbed his arms and held them firmly against his back while putting his knee on his lower back.

"Let me go! Is this any way to treat me? A Lord?" Lord Stansfield argued.

"If I had my way, you'd now be writhing on that sword, you worthless varmint." Raising his voice, Lord Somerset called for the butler. "You there! Come at once!"

The butler popped his head around the door, his eyes wide.

"Get the constable," he ordered him.

"If you get the constable, you'll be out of a job, Atkins!" Lord Stansfield threatened him.

"And if you don't, you'll be an accomplice to abduction." Lord Somerset said in warning.

The butler looked from one to the other and quickly made the wisest of choices.

A few moments later, the clear sound of a constable's pea whistle filled the air, and to Lord Somerset's satisfaction, the odious Lord Stansfield was taken into immediate custody.

Lord Somerset immediately tore the restraints off his sister and gathered her trembling body against his. "You're safe now, my dear."

She cried tears of relief, realising her ordeal was over, and clung to him tightly, burying her head against his chest, her tears quickly turning to sobs.

Lord Somerset let her cry, and when finally her sobs abated, he said, "We'll spend the night at a local inn, and tomorrow morning, once I've seen the constable, we will make for home."

He pulled her away and looked into her blotchy face. "I must ask, for the constable will wish to know, did Lord Stansfield violate you in any way?"

He held his breath, hardly daring to hear her answer, but thankfully, she shook her head. "No, brother."

He closed his eyes with relief. If Lord Stansfield had dared to do such a thing, he knew he wouldn't be able to contain the need for true justice, and that wouldn't mean time spent in a jail cell for the odious cad.

Clasping his sister's hand, he led her towards the door. "Let us get away from this house. It is a dark place indeed."

After spending the night at a comfortable inn and speaking with the local constabulary in the morning, Lord Somerset hired a carriage to take them both home to Thornfield. His own horse he had tethered to the carriage, as he knew his sister needed the comfort of his presence inside.

They spoke little on the way home, with Beatrice still distraught over the event and Lord Somerset not wishing to push her for the details. For the moment, it would suffice that she was in his safekeeping.

He stared out of the window vacantly, his mind focused on what would happen to Lord Stansfield now that he was detained. Would his vast wealth allow him to slip unpunished from the arm of the law?

His eyes narrowed. If so, he would press private charges against him. Lord Somerset had his own connections in London, and if it was the last thing he ever did, he would make sure that Lord Stansfield paid for his actions.

The carriage rolled through the gates at Thornfield, and when the house came into view, he looked up at the windows to see Genevieve and Isabella staring down at them, their faces anxious. When they spied Beatrice in the carriage, their eyes visibly widened, and even from that distance, he could see the relief.

It took but a few moments for the two girls to come flying down the front steps to greet them.

Isabella was the first to embrace his sister as he helped her out of the carriage. "Oh, dearest Beatrice! We were so worried about you!"

"Come inside, my dears, and we'll explain what happened." Lord Somerset said, ushering them towards the house.

With them all settled in the drawing room and refreshments ordered, Lord Somerset allowed Beatrice the dignity of explaining the circumstances of her disappearance. She was still clearly traumatised by the whole affair, and he hoped, in time and with her friends in attendance, she would put the horrendous episode behind her.

Drawing Isabella to one side, he asked her if she would remain at Thornfield for a few days longer.

"I should love to," she replied softly. "Not only to help Beatrice, but it will be nice to spend some more time with you."

He smiled and raised his hand to gently stroke her cheek. "Then it is arranged. I will send a message to Oakwood, informing them. Do you need any belongings brought here?"

"I don't, but perhaps Genevieve might." She looked over at her and Beatrice, still deep in conversation. "I shall ask her later at a more opportune time."

Isabella looked up at the strong man that would soon be her husband and marvelled at his demeanour. He had just rescued his sister from the arms of the devil, and yet he was so calm. She pictured the fight between him and Lord Stansfield, imagining what it would have been like to witness such an affair. For Beatrice, it must have been so frightening.

Isabella placed her hand on his arm, delighting in the feel of his strong muscles beneath the fabric. "You must be weary from your travels, my lord."

He smiled down at her. "A little, but it is nothing compared to how I feel about having my sister back home." His expression grew fierce. "What an ignorant, obnoxious, evil man Lord Stansfield is. Even after my warning, he still sought to satisfy his own desires."

"I can hardly believe it myself." Isabella whispered. 'Go and get some rest, my lord. We will look after your sister."

With gratitude in his eyes, he raised her hand and kissed the soft skin, making her blush. "What would I do without you, my love?"

Isabella's heart was fit to burst as he left the room. What a wonderful man he was, and with a thrill, she rejoiced in the fact that he was hers.

A few days later, Captain Harmon came to visit. Before he could see Beatrice, Lord Somerset took him into the study and enlightened him on the recent events.

At first he had been appalled, but then his expression turned to sheer anger, seeking retribution for Lord Stansfield's heinous act. He had been ready to rush to London and run his sword through the contemptible man, but Lord Somerset had managed to calm him down, telling him that the law was there to serve its purpose. They would deal with him however they saw fit. If not, he himself would deal with the matter.

Captain Harmon ran a hand through his hair, his face etched with worry. "How is your sister coping?"

"Lady Genevieve and Miss Hamilton have remained here to keep her company, and it has raised her spirits immensely. You will find all is well."

"I have something to ask, so I may as well do it now." He paused, suddenly looking a little nervous. "As Lady Beatrice's guardian, would you allow me the honour of courting her, Lord Somerset? I have grown to love her, and I hope that I can win her affection."

"I think she has already grown to admire you, Captain Harmon, and yes, you have my blessing. But go easy with her. She may still need time to recover from this unfortunate incident."

He nodded understandingly and then quickly set off in search of Beatrice.

Two weeks later, with not a cloud in the sky, Lord Somerset married the winsome Miss Isabella Hamilton.

"They both look splendid!" remarked Miss Eliza Harmon, her eyes softly watching the couple as they stood outside the chapel.

"Oh, indeed, a most handsome couple. To think our dear boy will be wed in only a month hence!" her sister Margaret replied.

"And to Lord Somerset's delightful sister, Beatrice. She is such a pretty girl, and her manners, so refined."

"What a wonderful end to summer, my dear." Margaret declared. "Now, I think we should make our way to the house for the reception. Lord Somerset set aside a carriage especially for us. So thoughtful for our old bones!"

Genevieve and Beatrice threw rice over the newly wedded couple, laughing gaily. "Oh, my, Beatrice, to think we two will experience this in a few weeks!" Genevieve exclaimed happily.

"What a summer it has been!" laughed Beatrice. "I will never forget it."

Linking arms, they followed the newlyweds as they made their way to the main house, where a lavish reception had been organised.

Beatrice, with the help of her friends and her dear Captain Harmon, was now much recovered from her terrifying ordeal. Lord Stansfield had been given a jail sentence of six months, and although she thought he deserved more, it gave her satisfaction that at least his crime had been dealt with.

She would never forget what happened but she could put it behind her. And that was all that mattered

A few hours later, with the reception nearly over, Lord Somerset gazed down into the beautiful blue eyes of his new bride. "I think it's time that we retire, my love."

He watched a becoming blush wash over her cheeks, and shyly, she agreed. Taking her hand, he thanked everyone present for a wonderful day, and with cries of joy and wishing them well, they left the large dining hall and headed upstairs.

This would be the first night that they would begin sharing a bedroom, and he knew Isabella would be nervous.

When they entered the bedroom, it was to find that Beatrice had strewn rose petals across the bed and decorated the four posts with pretty ribbons. Several vases filled with flowers perfumed the air.

"Oh, how beautiful!" Isabella exclaimed.

"Almost as beautiful as you." He declared. Closing the door, he could wait no longer. He swept Isabella against him, one hand cupping her face. His eyes glittered with a dark hunger, and a shiver of excitement rushed through him as he realised that she was finally his.

Isabella stared up at him, her desire for her husband clear to see. Although a little nervous, she trusted him completely and knew he would treat her with the care and love she needed. His lips descended over hers, claiming her with a mastery that left her almost breathless. His tongue sought entry into her warm, inviting mouth, and she responded fervently, lacing her hands together behind his neck and kissing him back with abandon. It felt so wonderful to finally explore fully the delights of lovemaking.

He broke away, his mouth kissing her chin and then the delicate curve of her throat. "Turn around." He commanded her softly. She felt his hands on her buttons, and then her dress pooled at her feet, her corset and bloomers quickly following. Clad only in her stockings, he turned her around, his eyes feasting upon her stunning beauty.

"You're so beautiful." He remarked, his eyes intense with passion.

She blushed alluringly, revelling in his admiration. Lifting her up in his arms, he placed her tenderly on the bed before quickly disrobing.

His gaze never left hers as he flung his clothes with careless regard onto a nearby chair in his haste to join her. He couldn't wait a second longer.

The bed dipped as he joined her and wrapping his muscular arms around her slender body, he proceeded to kiss her again, drawing a passion from her that she hardly thought possible.

"Ah, Isabella, my sweet, beautiful wife." He murmured against her inviting, softly parted lips.

He moved his hand to cup one of her breasts while brushing his thumb over the taught nipple. Instinctively, she arched against him, her body craving what only he could offer.

He caressed lower, over her softly curved hips, down to her perfect little bottom, and then, parting her thighs, he found the silky smooth entrance to her womanhood. His fingers explored her moist folds, softly awakening the sensitive flesh.

Isabella gasped softly when she felt his finger slide inside, the feeling was exquisite. He stroked her tenderly and she soon felt her body begin to soar. Her soft little sighs filled the air, seeking completion.

Suddenly, she felt his tongue against her hot, slick folds. She gasped, a little shocked at the intimate move, but when he began a steady rhythm, she soon felt her body soaring, seeking release from the intense assault. Soft moans fell from her lips as Lord Somerset continued his relentless quest to give her the utmost pleasure.

Lord Somerset could only wonder at his wife's passionate nature. He could feel her thighs tremble as she reached her pinnacle, and it was almost his undoing.

Willing self-control, he raised himself up and covered her slender body with his. Her eyes were half closed, and her cheeks flushed pink and rosy.

Guiding himself to her silken sheath, he entered her slowly. She was slick and ready, but even so, her womanhood was tight. Holding her firmly beneath him, he began pushing harder, and with a quick thrust, he broke through her virginal barrier.

Isabella gave a sharp intake of breath, and he quickly kissed her, murmuring words of reassurance and love, assuring her the pain would soon diminish. Slowly, he began to move his hips, gently at first, and then, when he felt her begin to move in time with his thrusts, he increased the tempo.

Isabella gripped her husband's forearms, revelling in the muscular strength she felt beneath her fingertips. His body moving against hers was giving her such exquisite ecstasy that she wished it would never end.

But soon, she felt her body begin to soar once again, every nerve ending responding to the pleasure he sought to give her. Suddenly, her body tightened, and she emitted a small cry as she reached her pinnacle, waves of pleasure washing over her heated body.

Lord Somerset continued to drive his hard shaft into her soft core until, collapsing over her, he filled her with his hot seed.

For a moment, neither moved, too replete and languorous to part. Finally, Lord Somerset withdrew and lay down next to her, cradling her in his massive arms. She snuggled against him and sighed softly, content beyond her wildest dreams.

He kissed the top of her head. "You are happy, my love? I hope I didn't hurt you."

Isabella looked up at him, admiring the hard line of his chiseled jaw. "Only a little, my lord but it soon passed. It was wonderful." She looked up at him, her eyes soft. "I love you."

Without a word, his mouth descended upon hers in a tender, hot kiss. When he finally raised his head, he said, his voice thick with emotion, "And I you. You will be happy here, Isabella. I will make sure of it."

Her eyes sparkled with desire. "Now kiss me again, husband." She leaned her mouth close to his. He didn't need asking twice. His hand entwined in her silky blonde hair, and he captured her lips, sealing their love forever.

The End.

About the Author

Maryse Dawson was born in England but now lives in western France with her family - a husband, three children and two cats. When she's not writing she spends her time visiting the beaches and surrounding countryside. She has always enjoyed reading romances and loves history so began writing a few years ago to include domestic discipline in her stories. An alpha male - a feisty woman and adventures that will keep you turning the pages!

Read more at https://www.facebook.com/maryse.dawson.5.